TOVE

No Ordinary Love

NEYREY

SEV·EN

/ˈsevən/

The number of completeness and perfection.
Oceans roll in seven waves, with the seventh being the biggest.
This is the seventh wave.

Chapter One

TOVE

"Lovie... wake up, Lovie." I felt myself being jolted from a deep sleep, as my body was being shaken awake.

"Daddy?" I slurred, eyes still closed and laden with sleep.

"Yes. Wake up, Lovie," he repeated while shaking me a little harder.

After a few seconds, my eyes fluttered open to study my bedroom, and I tried to recount where I was. My eyes then flowed to his eyes that seemed frantic, making my eyebrows dip.

"Daddy, are you okay? W-when did you get back?" I stammered. He had left me alone two days ago, to go on a business trip. He wasn't due back for another week or so. I had been managing fine and was instructed to only call him in case of an emergency, and there hadn't been one.

"N-no, daddy's not doing so good, Lovie." He continued to stare at me with those bewildered, dark eyes and dilated pupils. His hair was disheveled, and his tie was undone. "I'm not doing too well, and I need you to help me out."

"Huh? Yeah. Anything. Are you sick or something?" I asked, growing frantic myself. It had only been two years since ma's life had been consumed by cancer. If my father was sick, as well, I wouldn't know what to do.

"Y-yeah, Lovie, I'm sick. Not how ma was sick, but I'm sick," he said, as he continued to hold on to my shoulders, but his eyes glanced across the room. I scooted toward the headboard when I heard the heavy footsteps dragging across the hardwood floors of the hallway.

"Who is that? What's going on?"

"Times up," I heard from my door frame where a tall, dark figure stood.

"I—I just need another second." My father stuttered, as the figure flicked the bedroom lights on. He was a tall, slim, light-skinned man with dark eyes that looked black. He peered at me from the door frame, before a smirk played on his lips, and he took a few steps forward.

"Ain't no more time, nigga. Get'cho ass up and get her shit together!" the man demanded, as my eyes flew to my father, and my face contorted. He couldn't even look me in the eyes.

"Get my—what? What's going on?" I squirmed under my father's touch until he let me go and rose to his full height. His eyes glanced at me, and they were sympathetic, before he turned his head and walked away.

The man came closer to my bed, and I winced when he grabbed me by my jaw and looked, as if he was examining my face. "She is, as pretty, as you promised though. I'll give you that. Too bad her daddy ain't shit." He chuckled, but I didn't laugh, and neither did my father. Instead, he moved around my bedroom with his back turned to me. He grabbed a duffel bag out of my closet and began to stuff it with my belongings that were in my chest of drawers.

I snatched away from the man's grip on my face and jumped out of bed. I ran up to my father, as tears filled my eyes. I was so confused and scared, but he wasn't telling me anything.

"Daddy, what are you doing? Please tell me what's going on?" I pleaded with him, as he ignored me and continued to gather my things, as I pulled on his arm.

"I told you, I needed you to help me," he whispered, as he moved robotically, collecting my things, as I cried, and the man walked up to me, backing me into a corner.

"Hurry the fuck up!" he barked, making me jump and my eyes widen, as I started to sob. "And you, shut the fuck up!" he yelled, before yanking me out of the corner by my arm and holding me with a tight grip.

"Daddy... daddy, please!" I screamed and begged, as I fought against the man with all of my strength, but I was no match for him.

The man huffed in annoyance, before removing a gun from his waist and pointing it to the back of my father's head, making him grow still. "Didn't I say shut the fuck up?" he asked me, as I nodded and tried to stifle my cries. I didn't know what was going on or why my father was making me leave with the stranger, but I didn't want him to kill him.

"I'm so sorry, Lovie," my father said, as he glanced at me with tear-filled eyes, as he turned around and held my belongings out *toward the man. I wanted to scream; I wanted to cry out for him to save me, but the man had the gun trained on him.*

"Get ya shit, and let's go." He shook me by the arm, making me grab my belongings from my father. "Now dig in my pocket and give him his pay," he instructed smugly, making my eyes widen, as I stared at my father at the revelation that he was selling me.

"No!" I bellowed, as he struck my father across the face with his gun, making his head whip to the side, and his nose began to leak.

"Didn't I say dig in my fucking pocket? See, you gon' be a difficult one. But I don' broke the best of them."

"J-just get my stuff." My father stuttered, as he held his bloody nose.

I cried, as I shoved my shaky hand into the stranger's pocket. I pulled out something that I would learn later was an eight ball. My father was selling me for an eighth of cocaine. I dropped that packet into his hand, and he ran out of the bedroom, as the man let out a boisterous laugh.

"Them drugs will make a nigga do strange thangs, baby girl," he concluded while pulling me through the house, as I silently cried while only in my nightshirt and shorts. "Nigga ain't even get you no fucking shoes." He griped once we got past the threshold, before lifting me from the ground and carrying me to the black car. "Can't let my new girl get her feet fucked up. Niggas pay good money to fuck bitches with pretty feet. Then you sixteen too, with them pretty ass green eyes? Oh yeah, I'm finna make some racks off you." He grinned, before shoving me into the passenger seat of his car. I brought my knees to my chest in the front seat and put my head in my lap and began to sob so hard that my head started to hurt.

"Didn't I say shut the fuck up in the house?" I froze, as I heard venom drip from his tone, as the cold steel touched my temple. He kept the gun in place until he got settled and got the car started. "Don't make me shoot you, 'cause then I'mma have to go back and finish off yo' old man, since I would be taking a loss in profit. And Slim don't take no losses."

The rest of the ride to his house was quiet, as the car was filled with nothing but my sniffles. I figured that if my daddy was sick, then maybe he needed the stuff that the man named Slim gave him, and then maybe, just maybe he would come and get me. But I knew that if I acted out and Slim killed him, then I'd never have a chance. So, I was obedient.

"Don't get out yet. I'll get one of these hoes to get you some shoes." He grunted, before sending a text on his phone. He cut the light on in the interior of the car and stared at me pensively, before I hesitantly looked back. "You so fucking pretty I might just keep you for myself. Yo' old man said you was pretty, but not like this." I winced, as he slid a finger down my cheek. "Aw shit, calm down, Lovie." He said my nickname that my parents gave me, mockingly. "The way yo' old man snorts coke, he'll be dead in about a year, so the way I see it, you better off with me anyways," he said, before he rubbed my face again, but this time, I didn't move.

The door to the two-story house, down a secluded road, opened, and a girl in a mini skirt and bikini top tiptoed out while wearing stilettos. She frowned, as she approached the car once she saw me. "Don't think you gon' go in here makin' no friends, Lovie. Pretty girls like you usually don't. And don't trust nobody that lives here but me," he said, before getting out of the car, taking the shoes from the girl and *rounding the car. Who would've known that him telling me not to trust anyone would be the best advice that I ever received in life? The only thing he missed was to include himself, as well.*

Tap, tap

"You don't hear me talking to you, Lovie? Get yo' ass up and go fix my breakfast, before I have to go!" Slim demanded, after he tapped my face lightly. I sat in his bed naked, just how I had been trained to do since my first night there. I was caught in a daze, thinking about how I got there. How my father never came back for me, and just like how Slim said he would be, he was dead a year later.

I crawled out of his bed while he sat at the edge and stared up at me with his dark eyes watching my every move. I pulled on the silky purple robe and tied it taut, before he grabbed my arm and turned me to face him. He looked up at me with saddened eyes, before pulling me to stand between his knees. He sat there naked, as I looked him over, waiting for him to speak. I had learned that Slim was only thirty years old when he took me from my dad. And now at thirty-seven, he didn't really look any different. He was still slender but in shape, with buttery vanilla skin, a low fade, full lips that you could tell had darkened from smoking, and dark, almond-shaped eyes. The only thing that changed was that he had grown a goatee that he kept short and neat. Most women called him handsome and admired him the few times that we went out. He would always get upset because when he would look to me when they would compliment him or flirt with him, I wouldn't respond. I assumed that he wanted me to be jealous or to speak up and stake claim.

"I ain't mean to tap you in your face or nothing... I just kept calling your name, and you wouldn't respond. I mean, shit... you don't talk to me anyway, but you was just staring," he concluded, as I looked down at him a moment longer, before leaning over to give him a peck on his lips. I knew that that would get him to leave me alone and give him the confidence that he needed to not worry me to death all day.

He smiled up at me like I knew he would, before his hands slid up my thighs and to my waist. "You know I love you, right?"

I just stared at him... like I always did. Slim had kept his word on keeping me for himself the night that we met; well, the night that he bought me. He had spent seven years grooming me to be exactly who he wanted me to be sexually, physically, and maybe even mentally. He had strict guidelines on how he wanted me to please him, how he wanted me to dress, how much weight I gained or lost, and what he allowed me to listen to or be around. He even controlled how my hair was kept, which was why it was always a nuisance to me, as it hung at my waist. I had given him whatever he wanted from me except my voice. I refused to give him control over what I said, as well as what I did, so I didn't speak at all. My pleas to my father to save me were the last words that I spoke.

He sighed, before leaning his head against my stomach, as I just stared at him.

"Lovie..." he groaned, before lifting his eyes to meet mine.

"What do I have to do to get you to talk to me? I never hit you, I never let nobody else touch you, I buy you anything I think you might like... please... just tell me what I have to do?" he pleaded with me, as he did every morning. It was, as if he didn't comprehend how this situation came to be or, as if he didn't see anything wrong with it. I guess he figured that time would change things. "Can you at least tell me... tell me that you love me back? Do you love me, Lovie?"

Fuck no.

He sighed, before standing in front of me in all of his naked glory with his girth stuck to his thigh. "Just... just go get breakfast ready." He pulled my head back and kissed my lips, before releasing me. I leisurely slipped my feet into my slippers and left the room. I didn't miss the evil glares that I got from the other girls in the house, as I left the bedroom that I shared with him. Slim forbade them from touching me, unless they were doing my hair or talking to me, so I didn't care how they felt. He was right that I wouldn't make any friends. When I wasn't held up in his bedroom, I always heard them discussing me, and it was never pleasant.

I followed my usual routine and started to get his eggs, bacon, three waffles, and grits ready along with his Earl Grey tea that he enjoyed. It was a routine, so it wasn't long, before I finished fixing his breakfast and placed it on a breakfast tray, before climbing the spiral staircase with it. We had moved from that old two-story house long ago. He had made so much money from selling sex and drugs that we had moved into a mini mansion. That was one thing that the other women hated about me the most—they felt that I didn't contribute. But in my eyes, I contributed the most. I contributed my body and my life to Slim in a way that kept him satisfied and kept him from breathing down their necks. Before I came, he was taking advantage of all of them and beating them too.

He smiled, as he sat up in the bed naked and placed his phone down on the nightstand once I entered the room. I thought briefly about how I had never had the privilege of having a cell phone. My daddy thought that I was too young, and Slim figured I'd use it to run away. That was the same reason that he didn't give me any money unless I was in the store with him, and he knew exactly what I was buying. But the only thing I ever picked out for myself was books. I didn't care when he tried to shower me with expensive clothing and jewelry. None of it mattered more to me than reading. I felt like I had to try to keep my mind strong and sharp. At least that's what my ma used to say that reading was for.

"Have breakfast with me; you made enough for the both of us." He grabbed my forearm, as I tried to walk away after placing the tray into his lap. My vision fell to the floor, as I studied my toes and thought about how I needed them done again soon. The color on my toes was the only thing he would let me pick about my appearance.

I denied him every morning, but like clockwork, he still asked. "Go ahead and take your shower, Lovie," he said, before sighing in frustration and letting me go. My shower time was the only time that I got to be alone and not watched, or talked to, or glared at, or begged for my attention, or fucked. My shower time was the only time that I didn't have to be Lovie. I fucking hated the nickname; I always had. I was Lovie when my mother died. I was Lovie when my father sold me. I was Lovie when I was stupid and crying for a father that didn't love me and when I kept quiet to save his life, and I was Lovie when Slim raped me my second night here and broke me in just like he promised he would. I just wanted to be me and leave Lovie behind and down the shower drain, as I washed her off of me every morning. I just wanted to be Tove.

Chapter Two

JAHI

"Why do you always have to leave?" Caroline, Callie, whatever her name was, whined, as I glanced her way briefly, instantly silencing her. She knew that spending time with women, outside of sex, was simply something that I didn't do. The Nuru men weren't raised that way, and it was a reputation that we were known for. It was something that society now deemed, as toxic masculinity, but this wasn't that. We were raised to where we could have sex with, as many women, as we wanted to, but when it was time to settle down and fall in love, we settled down and fell in love with women from the motherland. So, anything else was simply for entertainment. And at the age of twenty-six, I was looking at three more years of entertainment, before my parents would return to the motherland to find me a wife.

After settling on what I would wear to this brunch, I left my closet to find what's her name gone and my maid, Barika, changing my sheets and fussing in her native tongue. I chuckled, knowing that she was the one who got rid of the chick for me. She was an older woman, who had come back with my grandparents many years ago and was their gift to me when I left my parents' home. Though my family had been in the states and me and my brother Khari had been born here, our family made sure that we were heavily connected to our roots. We knew the language, the history, and we kept the bloodline 'clean' by only having children with women from Africa.

"Thank you, Barika." I wrapped my arms around her full-figured frame, before kissing her cheek. She glared at me and swatted at me with a pillowcase, before continuing to fuss in Swahili.

As soon as I finished getting dressed, I was met downstairs by my assistant, Djimon. He was born in the states, like me, and his family was from Tanzania, as well. His family worked for mine.

"Jahi, we are going to be late. And your parents aren't going to blame their precious prince. They're going to blame the assistant that is supposed to have you everywhere on time," Djimon fussed, as I waved him off and continued out of the door, with him on my heels, going over meetings and deadlines for projects. Once my detail opened the door to the back of the Escalade, we were seated and headed to this family brunch that was held once a month. It was mostly a gathering where my family got together and just caught up with our busy lives. Every day was usually business, but for this one brunch, once a month, it was not.

"Jahi—"

"Mon," I spoke his name firmly, while slicing the air in front of me with my hand.

He huffed with a roll of his eyes, before staring out of the window. He knew that he was annoying me at that point. Sometimes I felt like my family assigned Djimon to me because I was laid back... unless I got angry. And typically, people didn't want to see me angry, so that was usually avoided. Everyone else was already so uptight, except Khari and me. Khari was just... There was no other way to describe him besides just saying Khari.

"Maybe unorthodox," I thought aloud, causing Djimon to give me an awkward glance, as we pulled up to the restaurant. I shook my head, as we pulled up to the small soul food restaurant that I knew was chosen by none other than my mother. As much as she was heavily invested in our culture, she loved American soul food just as much.

"Mkuu!" My father's loud voice boomed through the restaurant, as soon, as I walked in. I shook my head, as I went to greet him with a hug, before following suit and greeting my mother the same way.

"Well, if he's the prince, then I must be the princess," my older brother Khari sassed, as he sat back into his chair and crossed his legs, while making the elders at the table gasp.

"Must you upset everyone already, Khari?" I asked, as I sat in the chair that had been reserved for me, right next to him.

"You know me. The *shetani* has to stay busy," he tittered, making me do the same.

"Khari! Stop that now, boy! You upset the whole family with your mess!" our mother scolded in her thick accent. Though she had been in the states for many years, her accent always came through when she fussed.

"Don't upset your mother, Khari," my father added.

Khari gave a half-ass apology, before finding other ways to piss the family off. At first, everyone was upset because Khari was more feminine, which contradicted the way our family felt that Nuru men should be raised, and Khari chose to antagonize them with that. They were still trying to figure out what to do with him, as far, as arranging a marriage since he was almost the age for it.

"Jahi, when are you going to cut all of that hair, son? You look like a woman with your hair like that," an uncle insisted, as I looked at him dully.

"Well, I tend to like men that look like women," Khari interjected, before I could reply, making me shake my head, leading to my parents fussing again and him half-ass apologizing *again*.

After settling on smothered pork chops with gravy and rice, along with mustard greens and baked macaroni, I decided to sit back and let my loud Tanzanian family talk business. This was supposed to be personal, but the Nuru family didn't know how to not work.

"Is there anything that you would like to add, Jahi?" my father urged me to join the conversation, but I declined, making him huff frustratedly. Khari, on the other hand, always hopped in when it came to business. They didn't like how he lived his life, but they loved how he did business. I simply let the old heads run the business and ideas, and I stepped in to be the muscle or to deal with people that had decided that they didn't want to be compliant with the rules that we set. My father wanted to make sure that we would be fully equipped to take over his division when he retired, and when the time came, I would do so. I hadn't negated my responsibilities to be observant and learn the business. I was just quiet. I just figured it pointless to sit at a table with a bunch of men who figured they knew better than you, anyway.

What did the Nuru family do exactly? Any and everything illegal and legal, on a grand scale. Our hands were into any and everything that you could think of, and the law always turned their heads the other way because they were on Nuru's payroll. We had a colonizing mentality, and we took what we wanted. We were one of the most powerful families in southern Louisiana, and that said a lot to say that we originally weren't from this country.

As my family continued to discuss business with me adding in a word or two here and there to appease my father, I sat next to Khari, glancing out of the window at the quaint bookstore across the street.

"Baby bro—hmm," Khari hummed, while wearing a childish smirk, as he turned his head in my direction. He was confirming that he had seen what I had. "Well, what you waiting for, nigga? Go get her," he murmured and nudged me, prompting me to rise from my seat.

"I'm going to the restroom. I'll be right back," I told my detail, who was watching my every move. I could do whatever I wanted, but I didn't want my family in my personal business.

I walked into the direction of the restroom, before quickly making a left to leave the loud restaurant, filled with the sounds of native tongue mixed with English and silverware being clanked against plates.

As soon as I got outside, I caught another glimpse of *her*. She was still standing at the curb in front of the small bookstore, with several bags in tow, as if she was waiting for someone. I tried to hurry and cross the street, but it was lunch hour, so the traffic wasn't allowing it. I kept my eyes on the ochre-colored beauty, as her ride arrived. She was a type of beautiful I had never seen before, with wavy dark hair that flowed down her back.

"Ay! Hold up!" I called out to her from across the street, as she put her things in the back seat, right before she could dip into the car. That was when she finally glanced at me with those low, sultry, tantalizing eyes. Even from across the street, I could tell that they weren't brown by the way they contrasted against her warm ochre skin and dark hair.

Her face held no expression, as she glanced at me with no sense of recognition. I wasn't used to that because, not only did everyone know who the Nuru family was, females usually paid attention when I was around and followed my orders. I had finally been given the go-ahead to cross the street, and that was when she quickly dipped into the car, and the car sped off into traffic. I tilted my head, and my eyes widened in recognition when I finally paid attention to the car that she had gotten into. And that just made me further intrigued by her.

When I walked back into the restaurant, my family didn't even notice that I was gone. That's how brief our encounter was. But Khari knew, and he gave me a subtle smirk and raised an eyebrow in a way of nonverbally asking me what happened.

"I couldn't catch her in time," I mumbled, as I took my seat back next to him.

"Well, everyone has the one that got away, baby bro. I mean, I wouldn't know, but that's what I heard." He shrugged, before taking a sip of his cognac, causing me to side-eye him. It was then that it struck me.

"Baba, I do have something that I'd like to add," I intervened.

"Mkuu," he gushed, making me chortle. It was funny to see such a huge burly man that usually looked so angry, be so loving and doting to Khari and me. But to him, we truly were his legacies. "Mkuu has something to say!" he bellowed in that loud voice of his that sounded like thunder when he spoke.

"You remember that area on the East side where we were thinking about charging people to continue their businesses?" I asked, after everyone quieted down, and my father nodded his head enthusiastically. "I think that we should go through with that."

"But there aren't many successful businesses over there," another one of my uncles chimed in.

"Not legally, but illegally, there are. I heard that Slim is maintaining millions over there with the business that he runs with the drugs and the women," I recounted.

"But Slim is on a very low, low level, Jahi. It would be a waste of—"

"Jahi has spoken," my father interceded. "If my son, who has never failed us, thinks there may be something there, then we will start business in the East. We will move in on them, and they will pay us to keep their businesses going uninterrupted, as Jahi said. This is Jahi's first independent business venture, and we will support him in seeing it through," he spoke with finality, causing me to smirk.

Everyone went back to being loud and talking about the takeover of the East and other possible businesses that we could invade, by making them pay us taxes to keep running their business without us interrupting it.

I looked over to Khari, and his face held confusion for a while, until realization hit him, and he shook his head with a chuckle. "You a hoe. All of that for some pussy," he spoke lowly, before taking another sip of that cognac, and I shrugged.

I sat back in my chair and mulled over my thoughts of her. I knew that if she was with Slim, she was either a prostitute or had dealings with drugs, but for the moment, I didn't care. I wasn't even thinking about what I would do with her once I got her. I just knew that I was a man who was used to getting what he wanted, and at that moment, I wanted to acquire her. Slim simply couldn't keep her.

It was amusing to me that I'd never seen her before, being that my family had been to Slim's place of business once before, when we were contemplating taking over the East. And while he had a few nice-looking women working for him, there weren't any there that looked like her. Definitely none that a Nuru man would fuck, although we didn't take part in fucking prostitutes anyway. We never had to, and my family looked at it, as something dirty.

"Djimon, ride with Mika, and let me have a word with my brother on the way to his place." I heard Khari instructing our assistants to ride together.

"Now what on Mungu's green earth are you going to do with a hooker, Mkuu?" Khari's loud voice filled the back of the Escalade, as soon, as he hopped in. I grimaced.

"Will you keep your damn voice down? You may think our detail work for us, but they're just babysitting us for Baba and mama."

"You think I give a fuck about Craig going to tell Baba something? Craig don' sucked his own nut out of my ass before. I bet he ain't never tell them that," he said, referring to my driver, with a roll of his neck, as I grilled him.

"Too fucking much, Khari! Too much! You know that I don't care about you being gay, but with that shit, you went too far!" I fumed, as I pointed a finger at him.

He just stared at me for about five seconds, before he burst out laughing.

"Well, I'll no longer be the problem anyways once Baba finds out that the whole reason for your takeover was a prostitute. But I must give credit when credit is due, baby bro. She was a baaadddd ass bitch, and I could see that from across the street. Did you see how fine she was, even though she only wore leggings and that oversized hoodie?" he carried on, and I had no choice but to shake my head at him. My brother wasn't even feminine with how he dressed or anything. It was just his attitude and loudmouth that always gave him away— not that he was trying to hide it anyway.

"It's okay, though. I'll help you get the takeover thing all figured out since that's my specialty. But what you choose to do with her after that is up to you. She's just so damn pretty though. It makes you wonder how she even got caught up with a nigga like Slim," he fumed, with his face balled up.

"I don't know, and to be honest, I don't really give a fuck. I just know that I see something that I want, and if it requires taking her, then that's what I'm going to do." I shrugged.

"Wheww! That's what I'm talking 'bout, baby bro! That's how I'm ready for someone to be about me." This nigga took his time to roll the window down, before sticking his upper body out of it and screaming out of the window. "Come get me, baby daddy! I hate it here!"

"Get'cho retarded ass back in here!" I snapped, yanking his upper body back through the window. We were wrestling for about five minutes, before he decided to calm his ass down.

We sat across from one another with our chests heaving, as we caught our breath, before we looked at one another and started to laugh. See, most dudes had a problem when they found out that their brother was gay, and I didn't. I just thought it made this nigga Khari a little wilder and reckless with the shit that he said.

"All jokes aside though, I'm with you on this. And congratulations on your first independent venture, even though the premise is pussy," Khari joked, making our laughter start up again.

"Fuck you, Khari."

I just wish that I had at least gotten to know her name, I thought.

Chapter Three

TOVE

Please don't remember. *Please don't remember,* I thought, as I lie in bed next to Slim with my back turned to him. I paced his breathing, listening closely, as he deeply inhaled and exhaled, and I relished in it. I relished in each moment that he wasn't awake, each second that I could exist as myself and not who he made me be.

I inhaled sharply, as I heard the heavy breathing suddenly stop, and I felt the arm that he kept locked securely across my body, tighten. I closed my eyes to chant my wish of him not remembering, one more time.

Today was my birthday. It wasn't my actual birthday but a day that he, himself, had declared to be dedicated to me. Since I wouldn't speak to him or give him any details about myself, he decided on the day that he bought me with drugs, as my birthday.

He wanted to dedicate the day that he bought me with drugs to me, as my birthday.

"You know what today is, Lovie? It's yo' birthday!" he spoke enthusiastically, as he brought my body closer to his—if that was even possible.

Fuck.

I said nothing, of course, as he turned me onto my back, before climbing on top of me. My eyes roamed his features, as a grin covered his face. He leaned in to kiss my lips, as I reciprocated, before he tapped my thigh, signaling for me to spread my legs so that he could rest between them. His kisses trailed from my lips to my collarbone and on down, before his head eventually dipped under the covers.

I stared at the ceiling, as I always did and tried to imagine my old bedroom with the popcorn ceilings, before all of this. I used to lie in bed and mentally draw figures on them with the raised ceiling, as a guide.

"Door open." By the time Slim had my thighs propped on his shoulders, I heard the alarm sound.

"Lovieee!" I wanted to smile once I heard her calling out to me.

"Shit!" Slim hissed, before he could get started. He got out of bed with me doing the same. I slipped on my robe, as Slim simultaneously got dressed in his boxers and a t-shirt.

"Lovie!" She tapped at the bedroom door, as I took a seat on the bed. Slim frowned, as he swung the door open to let his little sister, Miranda, in. She was his only family that I knew of.

"What the fuck you comin' over here so early for?" Slim groused, as he glared at her.

"Shut the fuck up, Slim. I ain't here to see yo' ass, so don't worry about it. I know it's Lovie's birthday, and I wanted to take her out," she said, as her dark brown eyes fell to me.

She was tall, fair skinned, and slender, like Slim, except she had a little thickness to her hips and a nice, perky ass. She was pretty, and she was two years older than me at twenty-five years old. I honestly never knew how to feel about her. I never spoke to her ass either, but she was always fake nice to me. She'd bring me things for my made-up birthday, and she'd try to steal me away from Slim. She met me when I was sixteen, a few days after I had been taken away from my father, and she knew what her brother did for a living, but she seemed not to care. Or maybe she avoided it. Either way, in my eyes, she was sort of an accomplice since she did everything except help me leave him.

"Out? Lovie ain't going out unless it's with me. Plus, I want her to spend her birthday with me."

"So, you can keep her trapped in this bedroom and fuck on her all day? Don't nobody want that shit. You do that shit to her on the regular. It's her twenty-third birthday. Let her go out with me for a change. You can get on her nerves later."

My birthday was actually five months ago in January.

They fussed over me, as if I were a child.

"I don't do that! I—"

That was exactly what he did.

"Yes the fuck you do! I'm just taking her to go get some

books and to get some food, Slim. Damn! I'll bring her back."
She cut him off, as she fumed and glared up at him, causing
him to glare back at her, before sighing. He turned to face me,
causing her to do the same.

"Is that what you want, Lovie? You don't want to spend
your birthday with me? I was going to make you breakfast,
and we could've done something. I never spent your day
without you." He knelt, before me and pulled my hands into
his. His eyes roamed my face, as I just stared at him, before
looking to Miranda. I wanted to go with her so fucking bad.
She wasn't my friend or anything, but she wasn't going to try
to fuck me to death.

She gave me a smirk. "See! She looked at me! She wants to
go with me!"

My eyes fell back to Slim, and he looked as sad as he
always did when he tried to get me to speak. He sighed.

"I'll get her clothes ready. Go wait downstairs. She'll be
down in a few."

Miranda smiled brightly, before leaving the room. I
watched, as he walked in the closet and pulled out what he
wanted me to wear. It was the same thing he did every day. It
was May, and he was forcing me to wear a hoodie over the t-
shirt and leggings. I knew that was because he didn't want me
to appeal to anyone while I was out. He picked more fitted
things for me to wear when I was in the house with him, but
every time that I left, he pulled this shit. I went to the bathroom to try and hurry to shower and get myself together,
before he could change his mind.

After twenty minutes had passed, we were downstairs, with Miranda standing in the doorway waiting, as Slim held onto me tightly. He had never let me go anywhere without him before, and I could see in his eyes how terrified he was.

"I'm only letting you do this because you're turning twenty-three. Don't talk to anyone, and don't let anyone talk to you. You understand?" he asked, before kissing my lips.

"Miranda, I swear to God—"

"Shut the fuck up! She'll be back, just, as she left. Shit!"

"I'm going to handle something, so call me, before you get back so that I can know to be here waiting on her. Here's some money; buy her as many books as she wants."

"Okay! Bye, Slim! And I'm going to take your Beamer!" she quickly yelled, as she snatched the money from him, before she grabbed my hand and pulled me out of the door with her. He had a lot of cars, and she loved to drive them. But the Beamer was the one that he was most known for, with the weird metallic paint that looked different colors at different times of the day.

I sat in the passenger seat quietly, as she talked. She was talking to me and was answering herself since I wouldn't respond. Sometimes I wanted to talk back to Miranda, but I decided against it. I figured that if I said one word to her that her brother would try and use her as a conduit for our communication.

"I just don't see how you deal with his ass. He is sickening," she fussed about her brother. She spoke as if I had a choice.

Soon after, we were pulling up to a small bookstore that housed an even smaller cafe. I wanted to smile at the sight of it.

"Here we are. Lovie," she called my name, and I turned to face her. "There's nothing you want to say to me at all? Slim isn't around, and you can talk to me. I mean, we're practically sisters." She attempted to sound comforting. But I never read or heard of a sister that would let the other be held hostage. So, I just turned my head to face the bookstore. "Suit yourself." An attitude was apparent in her tone, but I didn't care. I didn't care about anything.

Once we walked into the bookstore, her phone began to ring. While she took the call, I took that as a chance to roam the store. I could read every page of every book in every store. The knowledge, stories, covers, and themes were so interesting. I picked up any and everything that I could carry in all different genres.

"This is some heavy shit," Miranda said, as she lifted a book that I had picked up, *The Republic* by Plato, and read the description. We were seated in the cafe section of the bookstore and had just finished eating. She ordered buttered croissants and coffee. I hated the taste of the plain black coffee. In fact, I didn't like coffee at all. I never gave objections, though.

I looked her over and wondered why she was so interested in me. I wasn't interesting. Shit, I didn't even talk. Maybe this was her way of reconciling with herself for what she knew about her brother's lifestyle.

"Well, since you got all of this shit, I'm going to pull the car around so that you can get in. And I know you won't piss me off by trying to run away or something." She raised an eyebrow at me, before continuing. "I don't want to hear Slim's mouth, and I know you don't have anywhere to go."

Bitch.

She rested her hand on top of mine and sighed, before looking like she was trying to choose her next words carefully. "I know he seems mean or like an asshole, and how you guys met was unconventional, but my brother really does love you. And I really do see you, as a sister. You never know, maybe he'll let you out more if you talk," she suggested, as she watched me a moment longer, before shrugging and going to pull the car around.

She was fucked up just like him to think that anything about this was normal or simply *unconventional.* I grabbed my three bags of books, as I trotted toward the door. I waited by the curb for her to pick me up, as I mulled over her words.

I should run. But where would I go? I have nothing. I have no one, I concluded.

She pulled up to the curb with loud music blasting, and I opened the back door, before dropping the books inside. I felt weird. I felt... watched. Not like the normal stares that I got when I was out with Slim, but something different. Something enigmatic.

"Ay! Hold up!" I heard faintly over the loud music that Miranda was playing. I looked across the street, and I saw *him.* I didn't know who he was, but he was... beautiful. Almost like the men that I would see on some of the covers of some of the magazines that I passed in the bookstores. He had thick, curly hair that was pulled into a loose, low bun, and light caramel-colored skin. He had a strong jawline, high cheekbones, and a sharp nose with a neat beard. He was even dressed like he was from a magazine, in nice jeans and a nice shirt with loafers.

"Lovie! Come on, girl. Let's go!" Miranda shouted, snapping me from my trance, forcing me to shut the back door and quickly dip into my seat in the car. I glanced her way to see if she had noticed him, but she hadn't, being that she was entranced in her phone.

Who was he? I thought. But then I quickly decided not to worry about it. It wasn't like he could save me or like I'd ever get to figure out who he was. I figured out a long time ago that I would be stuck with Slim until I died.

She had forgotten. She had forgotten to call Slim and let him know that we were on the way back. I wanted to remind her. I *should* remind her. I sat in the car, nervous as hell, as I stared at the house. Slim's car wasn't there, but the other women were. He didn't want me around them without him, and I knew he would be pissed if I walked in there without him.

Shit.

"Lovie, we're here!" Miranda snapped her fingers in my face, making me face her. "Girl, sometimes I think something more is wrong with you besides being mute." She chuckled while turning the car off and holding his car keys out to me.

"Well, this was fun. Give Slim his keys for me," she spoke, as I hesitantly got out of the car, before grabbing my books. I stood in front of the door, and my hand trembled, as I placed the key into the lock. I knew that Slim wouldn't hit me. He'd never done that. His punishment was releasing his anger through sex. Through *rape*. Nothing like how he was trying to be this morning. It was more aggressive.

I sighed, as I looked back and saw Miranda watching me attentively to make sure that I went into the house. Once inside, I shut off the alarm and quickly tried to go up the stairs, before I bumped into *her*. They called her Lani. She was Slim's favorite girl, before I showed up and the one who had brought me shoes my first night there. I had briefly made the mistake of thinking she'd be a friend to me when I got here or that she would help me, but her jealousy consumed any notions of that.

"Watch where the fuck you going!" she snarled. I just tried moving to the side so that I could go upstairs and lock the door until Slim came home, but she blocked my path. "Thinking you all fucking that. You getting beside yo' fucking self!" she spat. In that moment, I knew that *she* had purposely bumped into *me*. Before I could shield myself, I was being hurled down the stairs, as my books flew everywhere.

"Miranda fucked up today," I heard her say, as I was trying to get up, but my leg was hurt. I held a hand up, but to no avail, as I saw her foot, before it crashed down onto my face. She started to stomp me, as I heard feet starting to patter down the steps.

"Let's fuck this bitch up!" I heard another girl yell, before I briefly saw her and another girl jump in. I didn't know every girl's name. I tried to shield my aching leg, as they stomped me, punched me, and pulled my hair.

"What the fuck!" Slim bellowed, before coming up and swinging on all of them. I watched through swollen eyes, as he slung them around and punched Lani in her face, instantly creating a cracking sound. "What the fuck did y'all hoes do! I'mma kill you bitches!" he exclaimed, as he ran to me and grabbed my face, before his jaw clenched. The three girls that jumped me scattered and dispersed up the stairs together, as best they could. "Why the fuck didn't she call me!"

Slim scooped me into his arms and carried me up the stairs, kicking my books, as he cursed. Sadly, I cared about them more than what had just happened to me.

"Look what the fuck they did to your pretty face! I'mma kill them bitches." He was fuming, as he laid me onto the bed. I lay still, as he pulled all of the clothes from my body to examine the damage with his dark eyes.

"See why I don't let you go nowhere, Lovie? You see why you need me? You need me to protect you from everybody, just like I protected you from yo' daddy. See, you're special to me, and other people just gon' try to take us away from each other!" I stared into his angry eyes, as he glared down at my naked body. He took his shirt off to wipe my nose since it was bleeding.

He walked away for a moment, and I heard him cursing Miranda out on the phone and threatening her. When he was this mad, I knew where things were headed. I watched, as he approached the bed, naked, before climbing on top of me. I winced against my will when he spread my legs, and that caused his eyes to immediately flow to my face. His eyes lit up, and it was almost, as if he wanted to smile because I was finally giving him a reaction to something. I mean, shit, after all, I had never been jumped before. I closed my eyes, as he forcefully rammed his dick into me. My body jumped with his every painful thrust, as I grimaced because of my leg. Not the rape; that was normal for me—even the aggressive, painful version of it. It seemed, as if me grimacing and holding my eyes closed tightly made him fuck me harder, deeper, and more enthusiastically.

"I just love you so much. I can't ever let you out of my sight again," he groaned, as he heaved on top of me, and I gave it my all to not let my tears fall. How did he love me if he could rape me after that? After my body was battered and I still had dried blood on my face? I had never read a book about a love like that.

I took my mind to the pages of the books that I had read, as I spent the rest of my 'birthday,' as I always had since living with him; on my back.

Chapter Four

TOVE

Courtney. I squinted one eye, as I looked toward the ceiling with the other, as if that would give me confirmation.

No, definitely too masculine looking for a gender-neutral name. He looked like a... like a warrior, with those broad shoulders, puffed out chest, and sharp features, I thought, before my eyes fell back to the pages of the book of names and their meanings, in front of me. I had always been obsessed with names and their meanings. I always wanted to know if they correlated with that person's character. Slim's real name was Adiv, and that meant pleasant and gentle. To me, he was everything but that.

Maybe something Samoan. I quickly flipped to Hawaiian names, as I thought back to his huge stature, the caramel skin tone, and the somewhat loose, curly texture of his hair.

Male, Hawaiian, Kana, a Maui demigod who could take the form of a rope and stretch from Molokai to Hawaii.

Fitting but not quite.

I fell back on the bed and stared at the ceiling, as I closed my eyes tight and tried to wash the images of the stranger away from my mind. No one had been compelling enough for me to remember or think of after seeing them in these past seven years but him.

Who was he?

I sighed, before sitting up in the bed, figuring that I should probably go ahead and take my shower and get ready for bed, before Slim came home. He said he had a meeting earlier today and would be back but had yet to come. And I was excited for every moment that I got alone. Maybe if I fell asleep before he got here, then I could avoid him altogether.

After placing the name book back in the neat, alphabetical pile of books where I kept them in the corner of the room, I stepped into the bathroom and began to run the shower scorching hot—a tactic I'd learned so that Slim wouldn't follow me inside. I began to undress, and I wanted to see if my face had recovered from the beating that I got a week ago. I took notice of how my leg recovered quickly, as I went to stand in front of where the bathroom vanity used to be, before my eyes fell to my wrist. I stared at the raised welts on my wrist and smiled. I remembered last spring and the feeling of my soul ascending and leaving my body, as I bled out on the floor. It was the freest I'd ever felt.

I had locked the door and broken the bathroom mirror

with my fist, grabbed a piece of glass, and dug as deeply as I could, as quickly as I could, while Slim pounded on the other side of the door. I thought I was gone until I woke up tied to his bed with my wrist bandaged. Since then, the bathroom and the bedroom had been child proofed besides the bedroom door that he kept bolted to keep the other girls away from me. And when I went downstairs to cook him breakfast, he made sure to watch me from his phone. He had cameras everywhere in the house, to watch me and to make sure that all patrons behaved and paid their women of the night/dealers, as expected.

I quickly stepped into the shower and shut the door once I heard the bolts on the bedroom door being undone.

"Loviee!" Slim slurred, notifying me that he was drunk, hence him staying out late. I rolled my eyes.

"Loviee!" He kept calling my name, as if he didn't deadbolt my ass in here. I heard him running into the walls and staggering into the bathroom, as I started to soap my washcloth. I didn't even react, as the cool air filled my space. "Lovie," he called me softly, making my eyes roam to him, as I started to bathe myself. If I didn't look at him, he'd continue to call me.

He leaned into the shower with his eyes lowered, and his lips puckered, as he held onto the shower wall with one hand and a bottle of tequila in the other. He reeked of alcohol and that old man smelling cologne that he always wore too much of. I gave him a kiss, before he staggered to the closed lidded toilet and took a seat. He drank from that tequila bottle while watching my every move.

I'd closed my eyes and lifted my head under the shower head to let the water pelt against my face, when I heard him sniffling. I hated drunk Slim just as much as I hated angry Slim. Fuck, I hate *all of him*.

"Lovie..." he called me, as he cried. "I do everything for you! I give you every fucking thing, and you still don't love me." I started to rinse the soap from my body, to conclude this unpleasant shower.

"I buy you all them dumbass books. I feed you good, I know damn well that I fuck you good—better than I ever fucked any bitch before, and you still won't talk to me. Can you at least tell me that you love me? Please? I just need to hear it one time so that I can know that I'm doing something right with you." He cried from his soapbox, as I quickly dried off and wrapped the bath towel around me, before walking up to him so that I could help him get to the bed. I went to grab his arm, but he caught mine first and stared up into my eyes, as tears streamed down his tan cheeks. "Please," he pleaded, as if I'd ever give him the satisfaction. I looked to my left, as he pulled me into him and sobbed, as his head rested atop my stomach. I attempted again to grab him and pull him up, and this time he let me help him. I threw his arm over my shoulder, before walking him over to the bed.

"We leaving in the morning," he grumbled, but I ignored it because I didn't know what he was talking about. I grabbed the bottle of tequila from him, before I shoved him onto the bed, and he fell back in sobs.

While his arms covered his face, I quickly took the rest of the contents of the bottle to the head, as I felt the liquid burning through its path down my throat. He didn't allow me to drink, but when he was drunk, I'd finish whatever he had since he wouldn't remember if he finished it or not.

After placing the bottle on the nightstand, I stood over him and noticed that he was sleeping. I picked the bottle back up and twirled it a little, wondering if I struck him with it, would it kill him. But if I killed him, then what? He was all I had, and he had made sure of that. I never saw where he kept money, so I wouldn't have that.

I sighed, before placing the bottle back down and kneeling to take his shoes off. I was going to have to put him in the shower and get him ready for bed.

Crash!

My head popped up to see that Slim had sat up, letting me know that we had both heard the sound of glass breaking downstairs.

"The fuck!" he bellowed, before marching past me and grabbing his gun from the back of his waist. "Stay in here and pack some of our shit," he told me, before marching out of the door, forgetting to lock me in.

Pack some of our shit?

I was shocked. Even though this was a house where prostitutes stayed and drugs had been prepared and sold, the patrons usually behaved. And when they didn't, Slim would appear, and they'd calm down. Nobody fucked with him. He had made a name for himself early in this lifestyle, according to him and Miranda. And on top of everything else, this was a Sunday, the only day that we didn't serve nor service.

When I heard Slim yelling, I knew that shit had gone wrong, terribly wrong. He may have yelled at us, but never had he ever had to raise his voice when speaking to another man.

Or men? I thought, before creeping toward the door and hearing a variety of voices. I didn't know if it was curiosity or what, but that enigmatic feeling swelled in my chest, and I felt something pulling me downstairs.

"What the fuck are you doing?" Another girl, whose name that I didn't know, whispered harshly, as she grabbed my wrist. I looked down at her hand, before looking up and glaring at her until she let me go. I crept down the staircase, as I squatted down just enough to where I could see what was going on, but they couldn't see me.

It was... it was *him.* He was with two other men, one of them almost his height and the other significantly shorter. The man that was almost his height held an uncanny resemblance, as I assumed they were brothers.

What the fuck? Is he here for... me? I quickly released the thought when I heard him talking about a ransom.

Shit! I thought when his eyes were pulled to mine, and he did a double take. I was entranced by his stare. Looking into his eyes had me like a moth to a flame, before snatching myself out of it, when I saw him subtly tilt his head. I was quick on my pivot, as I tried to run up the stairs.

"Wait!" A voice—*his* voice, called out to me, as I heard a gun being taken off of safety behind me. I vaguely heard Slim begging and bargaining, before being told to shut the fuck up.

I closed my eyes and cursed myself, before opening my eyes and making sure that I felt them bore the glare that they always did. If I was going to be gunned down with nothing but a bath towel wrapped around me, at least they wouldn't get the privilege of seeing me afraid. I turned around to find the shortest of the three invaders with his gun trained on me.

Fuck.

Chapter Five

JAHI

ray? Blue—no. Green? Maybe hazel... I pondered on the chick that I saw leaving the bookstore and the color of her eyes. I wasn't close enough to get the exact color, but I didn't have to be close to notice that although she had light-colored eyes, something about them seemed dark.

"A bad bitch is here!" Khari marched into the boardroom at one of our many offices, where we conducted business. "Mkuu! I have to tell you about all of the fun I had last night!" he gushed, while I just sat there with my hands clasped together and stared at him. He shoved my shoulder and said, "Don't be that way, nigga! I'm about to help you get your mystery pussy, and you over there being all rude." He rolled his eyes, as I just shook my head, before looking at my watch. It was too early for Khari and his loud ass mouth and bullshit.

"So, I went to that new club *Rage* last night, right? And—"
He was cut off by my business partner, Deon Harmon, knocking, before walking into the office.

"Mmph," Khari huffed. For whatever reason, he didn't care for Deon. He said that he gave him bad vibes. I didn't care either way since this was all business. And if he ever got out of line, I'd just fill his ass up with lead. It wouldn't be the first, and I highly doubt the last time, since I'd had to kill someone before.

"What's up, nigga?" he asked, as we slapped hands.

"'Sup," I responded.

"Khari."

"Deon," Khari retorted, with a roll of his neck and eyes, causing Deon to chuckle. Deon wasn't from Tanzania like my family or anyone else employed by us. He was from here, in Baton Rouge, Louisiana. His family wasn't as powerful as mine, but he and his father had garnered enough recognition to be allies. They had a little power with law enforcement and old money. Deon was going to assist with the takeover.

"So, where is this shit bag at? I got stuff to do," Khari fussed, as he tugged on his Versace cufflinks and squirmed in his seat.

As if he had spoken him up, Djimon walked Slim through the door.

"Greetings, gentlemen," he spoke, as he walked over to where we were seated at the round table with an outstretched hand. While Deon and Khari shook his hand, I declined.

Something was off about the nigga to me. He seemed skittish, and Jahi didn't fuck with skittish niggas.

"Uh, okay," he said once he noticed that I wasn't going to accept his hand, and Khari raised an eyebrow at me while smirking. "How can I help you, gentlemen?" he asked, as he looked around with his beady, dark, frantic eyes, roaming about. It wasn't unusual for people to be afraid once a situation landed into my hands, because that typically meant death, but this was different. This nigga's character was flaw as fuck. It smelled worse than that cheap ass cologne he had on.

"You can start by having a seat. I don't speak to anyone standing over me."

"Oh, my bad, my bad. I just haven't heard anything from your family in a couple years, and I was curious as to why I was called to this meeting all of a sudden," he concluded while taking a seat across from me, as I just looked at him. I couldn't shake the feeling of wanting to snap his neck.

Khari sensed the tension and decided to take over. "So, just getting straight to the point. We've recently revisited the idea of taking over the area where your business is conducted, and we've decided to move forward with receiving taxes."

"But I thought it was determined that we weren't making enough money in the area. I mean, I make the most, and I ain't even doing that well. A few drugs here and a couple hoes there, but that's just enough to keep the lights on, re-up product, and feed the hoes," he said with his hands outstretched.

"Well, it sounds like you need to be shut down anyway,

since you aren't profiting from your business," I concluded, as his eyebrows tented. His eyes bounced from face to face, as he realized that we weren't moved in the least bit by his pity story. I was coming for what—who I wanted, regardless.

"Fellas, you know what? I may have a little something saved up to start paying the taxes. How soon are we talking?"

"Tomorrow," I replied flatly, making his eyebrows tent again.

"Well, shit, how much we talking?"

"Five million." That was Khari. He was the bargainer, and he always did hard research, before we moved into an area so that we would know what we were dealing with. He knew how much every business, legal and illegal made, and what was affordable.

He offered an uncomfortable chuckle. "Fellas, I'm a low, and I mean very low-level drug dealer and pussy pusher. I don't just have five million dollars laying around, and even if I did, that would be all that I have, and I wouldn't have enough to keep my business running at all."

"So, we should just smoke you now then?" I placed my Beretta on the table and leaned back in my chair. I wasn't one for negotiating, another reason why I stayed off of this end of the business.

Slim's eyes grew wide, before shaking his head. "N-no, no. I'll see if I can connect with some of my contacts and get an advance, so that I can have that to you gentlemen by tomorrow," he said through shaky breaths, as I gave a single nod.

"Leave," I instructed, as he slowly rose from his seat and left the room like a man on death row.

"Damn, your family going up on business tax or some shit? I've never heard y'all start off with five million, before unless it was a big corporation," Deon inquired, but I ignored him, as I watched Slim leave the building through the glass panes.

"We'll go get that ransom tonight to make sure he comes through on that five mil." I let my eyes flow to Khari once Slim had left the building. He nodded while wearing a smirk. We knew Slim made roughly two million a year, so we knew he couldn't afford what we were asking. We also knew that he would more than likely try to take off and start up shop some- where else instead of paying up, and I couldn't let him take off with my shit. I couldn't let him take off with *her*.

———

"Look at this poor, dumb, fool." Khari shook his head from the passenger seat, as we watched Slim stumble into his home, drunk. We followed Slim around all day, as he made various stops to try to gather the money that he needed. That wasn't going to work out for him, because the same alliances and connections he had were the same people that we had hit up prior to a meeting with him. So, we knew they were dry, but we followed him anyway to make sure things went as planned. After seeing that he couldn't get any loans, he headed to a bar.

Once we waited outside of Slim's place of business/home for five minutes, we got out of the car to meet Deon, who had already disarmed the alarm system. Deon rode along with us to go collect leverage for ransoms in the past, so him riding along with us wasn't out of the ordinary. He didn't know that we were here for *that* girl specifically. He just knew we'd take one for leverage.

"Ready?" Khari asked, giving me that childish grin. I just glanced at him and shook my head, before leading the way.

Crash!

Khari threw a brick through the large windows in the front of the home, right as my hand was on the doorknob. I turned to glare at him.

"You know I like the theatrics." He shrugged his shoulders, causing Deon to titter. I shook my head, before opening the door and walking through, as we saw a sobering Slim, running down the stairs, pistol in tow and only one shoe on.

"Ahh!" he yelled and grabbed his hand that I shot the gun out of. "What the fuck, bruh? What are y'all niggas doing here? I thought we had a deal set for tomorrow morning!" he yelled while he held onto his bleeding hand.

"We figured that we would stop by for some leverage to make sure you keep your end of the bargain," Khari revealed.

"Leverage? What kind of leverage? I know y'all don't want no drugs or no hoes, and that's all that I got," he cried.

"Hmm, what might Slim have that we may want for ransom, Khari?"

"I don't know, Jahi. What's valuable to you?" He raised an eyebrow, pacing with his gloved hands behind his back.

"I just said I ain't got shit but drugs and hoes. Y'all want one of those, then take it," he reasoned, as my eyes were pulled to the staircase for some reason.

Green.

After doing a double take, I caught green, low eyes peering at me through the iron bars, as she squatted while wearing nothing but a bath towel. I tilted my head subtly to get Deon's attention, before I saw her attempting to take off.

"Wait!" I bellowed, followed by the sound of a gun being taken off of safety.

"Wait, no! Not her! Y-y-you can have any of them except her!" Slim pleaded.

"Nigga, shut the fuck up!" I barked, eyes still on her, as she still had her back turned. I admired how the towel barely clung to her thick, buttery ochre-colored thighs and fat ass. All eyes were on her, as she slowly turned around, eyes dark and cold, as they pierced through Deon and then Khari and me. My jaw clenched at the sight of her having a black eye. I didn't even know her, and I felt that she was mine to protect. If he was putting his hands on her, then fuck this whole plan because I was putting a bullet between his eyes.

"You did that to her fucking face?" I asked through gritted teeth, as I yanked Slim from his place on the ground where he cradled his hand.

"N-no. The other girls jumped her!" he blurted with wide eyes, before confusion crossed his face. He was probably wondering why I gave a fuck.

"We'll take her."

"No, please. Any of them but her. She real young, and she

don't-she don't even talk and—" was all he got out, before I had my Beretta at his temple, as I stared down at him.

"Nigga, you think you got a fucking choice?" I grimaced. Slim was getting beside himself, thinking that I was going to bargain with him.

"No." He shook his head. "I was just saying that—"

"And I just don't give a fuck." I finished for him, before looking to her.

"Go put some clothes on so we can go, and don't try no weird shit," I demanded, making her eyes flow from the gun that Deon had trained on her to me. I wouldn't let him touch a hair on her head, let alone shoot her. But I needed to get my point across to Slim.

Khari had to grab me because I almost lost my shit when I saw her eyes flow from me to Slim, as if she needed his confirmation. He nodded at her with saddened eyes, and it was then that I realized that this nigga was in love with her.

As we waited for her to return, I could tell that Slim wanted to speak up, but he thought better of it, as he glanced between Khari and me frequently. If he had heard my reputation, which I knew he did, then he knew that I only came out to play for murking season.

I felt an eyebrow raise when she appeared at the top of the stairs while carrying several bags.

"Books," Slim spoke lowly, as he watched her come down the stairs while wearing an oversized hoodie and leggings, like when I saw her before. Her hair was pulled away from her face and on the top of her head, and the closer she got, the more I got pissed off, seeing her eye.

"She loves books. It's all she gives a fuck about, and she don't go nowhere without 'em," Slim continued to mumble.

"Deon," I signaled for him to go help her, and he met her halfway up the stairs to take the bags from her. I almost took his fucking head off when I saw him lick his lips, as he watched her ass while she descended the stairs.

"Mkuu," Khari chided lowly, to remind me that this was still a business situation.

"C-can I tell her bye?" Slim hesitated.

"Nah. Worry 'bout having that fucking money tomorrow morning, or you'll have bigger problems than a missing girl." He nodded, as his eyes misted over, but she never turned around to face him. She kept her back turned to us, as she waited by the door.

"I'm coming for you, Lovie," he called out, as we were leaving. I turned around quickly and rocked his ass so hard that he hit the ground. He groaned, as he lay there with his legs rocking back and forth. I didn't see what other niggas saw in him. He was a bitch to me.

"Calm down, Jahi Nuru!" Khari barked, as I was trying to go in for another blow. Slim was testing my patience.

"Calm down? You know who the fuck I am? That nigga is being disrespectful!" I yelled, as Khari glanced behind me, making me do the same. She was standing there with her back to us, as if she didn't hear anything going on behind her and was waiting for her next order. She was somewhat robotic, and I didn't like that.

"You got who you came for. Your temper is bad for business, Mkuu. You can't kill everyone that questions you or begs to be reasoned with anymore. This isn't that end of the job. If we were only menaces, we wouldn't have the respect that we do." He cupped my shoulder, and he spoke to where only I could hear. These talks were something we frequently had because of my temper.

"Let's go," I ordered, as I stalked toward her, towering over her short frame. She couldn't be any taller than five feet five, and that was short as hell compared to my six-foot-four frame.

"I can keep her or bring her home for you," Deon offered, making me mug him. "Or not." He raised both hands in surrender. After Deon placed her books in the back seat, I told her to climb in, and she did as she was told, only letting me catch glimpses of her eyes here and there, but I wanted more though. I wanted to be consumed in her and to know her and her story and why her eyes were so light yet dark. I wanted to unravel her, and I didn't know why. I'd never wanted to unravel anyone, nor had I ever cared about much before, especially not a woman, being that my fate was already determined.

The ride to my home was quiet with Khari only talking to offer her food or water, but she just stared out of the window, so we took that, as a no. Even Khari was quiet for once, as he sat in the passenger seat with that dumbass smirk tugging at the corners of his lips.

"Be kind," Khari urged me, as we got out of the car and shut our doors. She sat in the back seat like she was waiting to be told what to do again.

"The fuck you talking 'bout? I'm always kind." I frowned.

"No, you aren't, and especially not to women, Mkuu. She's different. I can tell. So, be kind to her." He lifted a brow, as he spoke, but I waved him off, before he rolled his eyes and went to his car.

I opened the door for her, and she just sat there looking ahead. I didn't know what to do with her and this robotic shit.

"Come on," I instructed while placing my hand over her soft, small hands once I saw her reaching for the bags of books. "I got that."

I opened the door for her and sighed when I realized that I was going to have to tell her to do everything.

"Come on," I instructed again, as she followed me through the house. Barika was asleep by now, so I kept quiet, as I headed straight to where the bedrooms were on the third floor. "So, this is my bedroom, and you'll be—" I was cut off by her walking past me into my bedroom.

I watched with my jaw dropped, as she instantly pulled her hoodie over her head and started to get undressed.

My eyes roamed from her pretty, petite feet to her toned calves and slowly up to her thick thighs and wide hips that narrowed at a small waist that was neither toned nor fat. It was just smooth, flat, and covered in that buttery ochre skin. Her body measurements were equivalent to the perfect hourglass.

My eyes lingered at the dip and dimples in her lower back. It wasn't long, before she was ass naked, as she climbed into the center of my bed and sat with her legs crossed, before lifting her eyes to meet mine for once. I had no choice but to be entranced by her facial features that held dark, neatly groomed eyebrows and dark, long, eyelashes, with a small nose that was rounded at the tip. Her Cupid's bow led to pouty mauve colored lips. My eyes narrowed in on that black eye, and while it didn't take away from her beauty, it angered me. It was out of place and never should've been there. It was then that I made a mental note to figure out exactly who did it and to handle them.

She just stared at me with a gaze that I'd only seen in a dead man's eyes. I only knew that she was still alive because of the rise and fall of her perfect breasts.

She was beautiful, and had any other woman done this, I would be in-between her thighs, but this wasn't right. This felt off, like Slim had her like a trained hoe, and that bothered me to my core.

"Say, look, I don't know how shit goes over there, but I ain't tryna fuck you. I was trying to tell you that you gon' be sleeping across the hall." I pointed at the door behind me, as I still stood in the doorway. If I was going to fuck her, she definitely wouldn't be fucking me out of obligation. It would be because we were on the same page, and we wanted the same shit. Pussy was a dish best served at free will. Anything else was creep shit.

She glanced behind me, before her gaze fell back to me. She wore no expression on her face, as she got up and scooped her clothes from the floor, before pulling them back on.

She followed me across the hall, and when I opened the door for her, I watched her, as her eyes traveled across the room, before she turned to me and looked toward her bags of books that I carried. No mouth gaping or amazement on her face like when I brought other women to one of my homes or condos. I had several, for different reasons, but this was my main home. This one was the grandest in appearance. And no nothing from her. All she wanted was her shit, so I set it down on the desk that was in the bedroom, before she turned her back to me again.

I knew that Slim said that she didn't speak, and I was now a living witness of that, being that she hadn't said one word to me, but I just had to ask. I had forgotten the name that I heard Slim call her.

"Aye. What's your name?" I queried, without really expecting an answer.

She looked over her shoulder, and for the first time tonight, her face held an expression. She didn't even have an expression on her face with a gun being held to it, but now she wore one. She looked confused with her eyebrows dipped, as if I'd spoke to her in my native tongue. I was almost ready to leave and be done with her for the night, when I heard her speak.

"Tove," she drawled in a heavy, country accent, riddled in sultriness. Nothing light nor airy about it. I instantly knew that her accent wasn't from the city.

"Tove," I repeated, but she had already given me her back again by then. I nodded to myself, before leaving her to herself and shutting the door behind me.

What the fuck did you just do, Jahi?

I thought that retrieving her might've been the most complicated part of this, but now I knew that it was going to be trying to get to know her. Trying to get to know *Tove*. And to make shit worse, I didn't even know why I wanted to.

———

Three days later...

Breakfast was a disaster. I stood outside of her bedroom door, as I contemplated going in there to apologize. But I didn't do that shit. *Apologize.* I didn't apologize to anyone. If anything, she was overreacting and needed to apologize to me.

I sighed, before reaching for the knob, but right as I did, Barika appeared out of nowhere and swatted at my damn hand with a damned pillowcase and began to call me everything but my name—in Swahili of course. I watched, as she entered the room and I tried to peek around her to see if I could see Tove, but she quickly slammed the door in my face.

Barika loved Tove's mean ass. I thought that she would treat her like any other female guest that I had, but she didn't. She said she loved that Tove stayed to herself and didn't sleep in my bed. She didn't mind that whole mute thing at all.

I pulled my phone from my pocket and shot Khari a text, before leaning against my bedroom door that was across from hers. I began to mull over this morning's events.

I had grown frustrated with Tove not talking to me. She went back mute after telling me her name. She didn't do anything except stay in that bedroom, as Barika brought her breakfast, lunch, and dinner. Since she didn't bring anything but books, I had a personal shopper to bring her some comfortable shit like what she came in.

I was trying not to stick my hand up her ass like a sock puppet, but this morning I had decided to use that obedience feature that she had. Bad idea. Terrible idea. She did, as told but in a stubborn way. Like she would do whatever was asked of her, but she was an asshole with it because she wouldn't speak while doing it. And if you asked for her attention, she would slowly give you those dead green eyes.

"Tove," I tapped on the door lightly. I knew that she wouldn't respond, so I just shouted from the other side what I wanted. I knew she was awake because I had heard her moving about. "Come down-stairs for breakfast in ten minutes," I demanded.

I stared at the door for a few seconds, as if it would respond for her, before retreating to the dining room table. Barika had prepared breakfast, as she did every morning that I wasn't on the go, and

Djimon was already seated at the table with his iPad, ready to tell me what I needed to handle today and the rest of the week.

After I took my seat at the head of the table, I looked at my watch to see how much time had passed. Only five minutes had passed, so I decided to give her the rest of her five minutes, before going back to get her.

Those were the longest ten minutes I had ever lived, as I checked my watch every second.

"Also, you have lunch with your mother and father tomorrow. Khari won't be joining you. He'll be out of town," Djimon ran off the to-do list, as I halfway listened.

Ten minutes. I had looked at my watch, and ten minutes had passed. I was sliding my chair from the table, as Djimon kept talking when I heard her feet start to patter down the stairs. I nodded appreciatively, as I watched her walk by in the leggings and tank top. She turned around, and her gaze fell to me, and I realized that she was waiting for me to tell her where to sit. I nodded to the seat directly across from me. I wanted to see all of her. I was relieved to see that her black eye had healed completely.

"Also—"

"Mon, it's time to eat," I interrupted him, prompting him to sigh, before putting the iPad to the side. I watched her, as she just stared at the empty plate before her, before Barika started to pile it up with bacon, eggs, and grits. I'd asked her to keep it strictly American when preparing food for Tove since I was sure she'd probably never had a Tanzanian meal before.

Once all of our plates were filled and Barika took a seat herself, at my urging, I bowed my head to say grace.

"Tuombe—" I was interrupted by the sounds of Tove's fork clanking against her plate, making me look up at her. She was eating, before prayer, and I found it disrespectful until it occurred to me that I wasn't speaking English. "We're saying grace, Tove. Tuombe means let us pray."

She continued to eat and ignore me. My head cocked to the side, as Barika and Djimon looked on with wide eyes.

"Tove, put the fork down so that we can pray over our food."

She put the fork down and chewed for a while, before looking up and swallowing while giving me those dead eyes.

"What? You don't thank God for the food you eat every day?"

She glared at me, before turning her head.

"Tove."

She slowly let her eyes fall on me again. Green eyes piercing through me.

"You don't thank God?" I repeated. I was sick of this mute shit. I didn't know what Slim did to her, but I wasn't that nigga. I was Jahi Ife Nuru.

"There ain't no God." Tove drawled, making Barika gasp and hop up from her seat at the table and start to pray in Swahili. My mind immediately began to fixate on how she pronounced God, as Gawd, but I quickly shook my mind from its fixation.

"Why do you think that?" I leaned forward, intrigued by her opinion.

She said nothing, as her gaze fell elsewhere.

"Tove."

Her eyes met mine again.

"Why would you say there is no God?"

Djimon looked between us. I guess he was feeling the intensity, as his eyes kept switching from her to me.

No response.

"Talk to me!" I bellowed, reminding myself of my father with his naturally loud and thunderous voice. Barika gripped her chest, before coming to swat at me with a towel, and I ignored her.

If Tove's face could possibly get anymore flat, it had. I watched, as she shot up from the table and headed toward the stairs.

"Stop," I commanded, making her halt in her stride.

I couldn't find it in me to order her to sit back down. I didn't like this bullshit, but I assumed that she was this way because of Slim, and again, I was not him.

"Go ahead."

She left, before I could watch her walk away.

And now I was standing here, leaned against my bedroom door, and wondering if I should go and apologize to her stubborn ass. I was surprised that Barika wasn't upset with her and was in there probably changing her bedding.

My phone vibrated in my hand, causing me to look down and read the message from Khari, before heading downstairs to open the door.

"Where is she?" Khari exclaimed, as soon as I opened the door for him. His ass had three other people with him. He had one person with a rack full of clothes, shoes, and purses, all dressed in plastic, and two people with black kits in tow.

"What the fuck is this, Khari?" I grilled him, before he took off his shades and looked me up and down while pursing his lips.

"The Calvary. That's what. Now move and tell me where she is. You know what? Never mind, I'll find her myself. Barika!" He marched off with the three people following behind him.

I followed them upstairs where Barika had led him right to her bedroom door.

"Tsssss!" Khari hissed. "I told yo' ass to be kind," he snapped at me, before marching into the bedroom with the three people, kits, and clothes rack following him. I tried to get a peek at her again, and again, Barika frowned at me, before slamming the door in my face.

I waited outside of the door for Khari to come out, saying that he had gotten the same results that I had for three days. I listened, as I heard him saying something that I couldn't exactly make out through the door, before it got quiet.

Oh fuck nah!

I rushed to open the door, when I heard her respond to him. When I opened the door, the whole room was quiet, as everyone glared at me besides Tove. She stared at Khari.

"Get'cho ass out!" he snapped.

Before I could respond and kick his ass out of my house, Barika was shooing my ass out of the bedroom, before shutting and locking the door.

I was pissed off. Nobody treated me how she was. I was Jahi Ife Nuru, sometimes Mkuu. And I ain't even do nothing to her ass. If anything, I thought that I was saving her from Slim, prostituting, selling drugs, and whoever beat her ass. I briefly pondered on if she missed him, but that thought made me want to go find him myself and kill him. He had skipped town just like we suspected he would.

Ain't this some shit, I thought, as I heard her thick accent through the door. I decided to go to my office and finish going over my itinerary with Djimon, before I hurt Khari, Tove, and maybe even Barika's ass.

Chapter Six

TOVE

I ran to the bedroom that I had been occupying as fast as I could, before shutting the door and diving face forward onto the bed.

He was a tyrant.

He was bossy, and I regretted talking to him.

I didn't know what it was exactly that made me tell him my name that night. I suppose it was a mixture of things. Grateful that I didn't have to deal with drunk Slim, grateful that I wouldn't get raped, grateful that I got to sleep alone for the first time in seven years, and I was confused, most of all.

I was confused because he asked me my name. As long as Slim had me, he had never asked my name. He and Miranda had automatically resorted to calling me Lovie, and the other girls called me bitch.

I don't even know why I spoke to him at the table. Maybe

me being grateful again or maybe that enigmatic feeling I had in my chest every time that I was around him. I always tried to ignore it when he would attempt to talk to me or when I was around him because he wasn't much different than Slim. He was using me for personal gain, and I cursed myself for assuming otherwise when he broke in, and I briefly thought that he was there to save me. I knew better than to think that, because nobody gave a fuck about me.

My body sunk further into the huge bed, and my eyes rolled to the back of my head because this bed was amazing. Everything here was. It looked like something that I saw in a book once before. Huge rooms, long hallways, beautiful expensive-looking furniture, and ceilings with crown molding edged in gold. And when I looked at the ceiling at night, I was greeted by a beautiful chandelier that glistened in the night light that seeped through the windows. This was a castle, the tyrant's castle.

Another reason I had declined to talk more to the tyrant was because I couldn't get used to this. Slim would get that money, and he would come back for me. Just like the time that I tried to run away about a week after being there. He found me, before I could even get down the street, and threatened me with a gun to my head, saying that he would rather put a bullet in my head than let me go.

My head turned to the side when I heard the door open, and shortly after, the short, round, brown lady came into view. She kept yelling the word Barika to me when I first met her, so I assumed that was her name.

"You okay?" she asked in an accent that was so thick and hard to distinguish, that I had to let the words roll over in my mind, before I realized what she was asking.

I nodded my head, causing her to smile, before she started to dust the room.

I didn't talk to her, but I wouldn't disrespect her and not give her anything at all. She was the nicest, most genuine person that I had ever met. On my first morning here, she ran me a milk and honey bath and worked on my black eye while I sat there and soaked. After that, she washed my hair with some concoction, and it was the softest and silkiest my hair had ever been. She also brought me all of my meals, when I declined the offer to join the tyrant.

"Ready?" she asked, as I nodded again.

I wasn't comfortable with her changing my sheets and cleaning up after me all by herself. I didn't make much mess, but she wasn't my servant. I knew how it felt to be someone's servant. So, I stood to help her change my sheets, and we moved in the same rhythm that we had the past two days. She was stunned the first time that I grabbed the other end of the sheets to help her.

After stripping the bed, she sprayed something on the mattress, as she did all of the time, and it made the whole room smell like melons. After that, we made the bed.

Pillowcases. Fitted sheet. Flat sheet. Plush stark white comforter. Duvet.

Right after we finished, I picked up a book, before taking a seat on the edge of the bed. She approached me with a warm smile that I hadn't seen since my mother's last days, before placing a hand to my cheek.

"He yells, but he means well," she spoke to me in broken English, and I just offered her a smile. I was here, as a prisoner of ransom, so I couldn't attest to those words.

I almost jumped out of my skin when I heard a familiar voice yelling her name. She scurried out of the room, before appearing moments later with four more people. She had slammed the door again, so I assumed that he was outside of it.

There stood one of the men who was with me the night that I was taken from Slim, and three women, all dressed like people from magazines. I took in his appearance, and everything about it said money, just like the tyrant. Even in simple clothes—shorts, a t-shirt, and tennis shoes, all seemed of fine quality.

"Khari Barbie, sorry I didn't introduce myself the other night. Business shit," the tyrant's look-alike shrugged, before handing his shades to one of the women behind him. They looked almost similar except he might've been an inch or two shorter. Probably six feet three, albeit shorter, he still towered over my five-foot-five frame. His complexion was darker than his brother's, making him the color of cinnamon. And while the tyrant had long, thick hair and just a beard, Khari sported a brush cut and a neat goatee.

"Okay, Miss Thang. We've got country chic, classy hoodrat, plain ol' classy, a little bit of sassy and a lot of expensive," he said, as he raked through the rack of clothes, shoes, and purses, before facing me. "I grew up in a strict family that believed that men should be men, so a nigga never had a baby doll until we got your beautiful ass. And this shit," he pointed at the clothes behind him. "Was expensive, so one of us is going to wear it, and since Khari doesn't wear fem gear, it's going to be yo' fine ass. Now I know you don't like to talk, but I don't like to talk to myself. And I'm not putting you in anything that you don't like, so we're going to need a verbal relationship, and I'm going to need your name. Mmkay?" he spoke, as I just stared at him, trying to take all of him in. He didn't seem this feminine the night that they took me, and he definitely didn't dress the part, but he was all sass and neck rolls right now.

I just gave him my signature glare, but he wasn't fazed because he pursed his lips and cocked his head to the side.

I looked to the expectant faces of everyone else in the room, before my eyes fell back to him, and he cocked his head to the other side, widening his eyes. I felt uncomfortable, yet his energy wasn't bad at all; it was...genuine, like Barika's. He didn't seem like an asshole like the tyrant. He was also the nicest to me out of the three who took me. He didn't yell at me nor hold me at gunpoint, and he was the one who offered me food on the way to the tyrant's castle.

"Alright, my name is Tove," I finally let out, forcing him to break out into a beautiful grin, before my eyes roamed to Barika's full face. "And I'm sorry for disrespecting your beliefs at the table," I told her, making her smile, before waving me off and telling me no worries.

"Well, I be damned. She speaks, and it sounds like sex." Khari shook his head while smiling, before the tyrant burst through the door. I kept my eyes on Khari.

"Get'cho ass out!" he fussed at his brother, and Barika went to work, shooing him out of the room in another language, before slamming the door in his face.

"Well, what y'all bitches waiting for? Get to work!" He snapped his fingers, and the three women instantly went to work. One was pulling out nail equipment, another hairstyling equipment, and the other started to organize the clothes, as Khari ordered them around.

It wasn't long, before I was forced to take a seat with one person giving me a pedicure and another standing behind me, as Khari pulled up a chair and sat next to me. Barika had left the bedroom.

"So, what are we thinking hair-wise?" the hairstylist asked, as she ran her hands through my long hair and gently massaged my scalp. Khari looked to me, waiting for an answer. I had never had a choice before. Slim always made one of the other girls do my hair, but he kept it long.

Slim.

He was going to be pissed and take it all out on me. I may as well enjoy myself while I could.

"Cut it."

"What?" the hairstylist asked with a gasp.

"You heard her. Cut that shit." Khari smirked, before leaning forward. "Where you from?"

"Where you from?" I retorted.

"Sassy. I like that. Mkuu is going to need that."

"Who?" My brows dipped.

"Mkuu—wait, you may know him, as Jahi," he surmised.

"Whom?"

Khari's eyes narrowed, before he rolled his eyes.

"That asshole has had you for three days and never told you his name?" he asked incredulously.

"Yeah, no name," I said, as I watched the first chunk of hair fall to the floor. It felt exhilarating.

"I'd ignore his ass too! The nerve! Men, tssss." He hissed, making me chuckle.

"She laughs, too." He smirked. "I'm from here, but my family is from Tanzania."

"Africa?"

"Mhm. Now you, because this accent is heavenly." His eyes rolling upward at 'heavenly'. He was so animated.

"The bayou. Delacroix, Louisiana."

"The baah-yoo," he exaggerated, I assumed to mock me. "I love it. How old are you?"

"Twenty-three, you?"

"Twenty-eight." His brows dipped, before his next question, and his face turned serious.

"How long you been working for Slim?"

"Seven years. And I didn't work for him. I was sold to him, and he kept me all to himself," I said, as I looked off, before my eyes met his again. He looked sad, a feeling you wouldn't think that he could experience with all of his upbeat energy.

"Sold by who?"

"My father. He was an addict, and I assume I was the only asset he had left." I watched the woman giving me a pedicure, and I noticed that she had paused, and so had the hairstylist. I glanced to my left, and I saw that the stylist stood there with her mouth gaped. My eyes roamed to Khari's face, and I saw tears budding in his eyes. "Don't cry for me. I stopped a long time ago."

"You deserve to cry a Red Sea of tears," he spoke seriously before he swiped at his tears that fell and snatched me into a hug. I wanted to resist any affection, but I couldn't. He wouldn't let go until I hugged him back. And I had to admit that it felt... warm. I felt something I hadn't in a long time. I felt safe.

"Tove."

"Mhm."

"You ever been to a crawfish boil?"

"I can't say that I have. No family or friends to do those things with. And Slim kept me in the house besides the occasional bookstore visit."

"Let's get her some casual outfit choices out," he instructed the wardrobe stylist. "I'm going to introduce you to my crew. Get you out of the house for once." He smiled at me, and it was so contagious that I had to give him a smirk.

"Khari?"

"Yes, gorgeous?"

"Can this conversation stay between us?" I didn't want Jahi knowing anything about me after how he yelled at me.

"Oh, honey. My lips are sealed. Jahi is going to have to do

his own hard work and prodding," he assured me, as he sat back and crossed his legs.

I thought for a moment about how I had never seen the names Jahi nor Khari in any of those name books.

"Khari?"

"Yes, beautiful?"

"What does Khari mean?"

"It's Swahili. It means kingly, albeit I've always been quite a queen." His hands formed a crown, as he placed them atop his head, forcing me to chuckle. "Why do you ask?"

"I've never read it in a book. And I sort of have a thing for names and meanings. I want to know if people are anything like their names."

His eyebrows shot up, before that perfect white smile graced his face again. "And she's a thinker. You're going to give Jahi a run for his money," he spoke. His tone was filled with amusement. I didn't know what he was talking about, neither did I ask. I had done enough talking for a while. Hearing my own voice actually sounded funny to me after being silent for so long. I pondered on how Khari's friendship seemed nothing like Miranda's.

After getting dressed in the high-waisted denim shorts and a black shirt with Medusa on it, I slid my feet into some black sandals that I couldn't pronounce the name of and admired the red color I'd chosen for my toes. I had only gotten a clear manicure on my fingernails. I never really liked getting color on them. I walked up to the mirror, and I couldn't help the smile that spread across my face. My hair was still in its wavy texture—since Khari was obsessed, and that was fine by me, but it was at my shoulders, and it wasn't heavy anymore.

"Thank you," I told Khari, as he stood behind me in the mirror.

"No, thank you."

I didn't know what I was being thanked for, so I just looked around the room, waiting for him to lead us out.

Before we could file down the stairs, we had to pass by what looked like an office, where Jahi had been with the man that talked way too much.

"The fuck?" I heard him mumble, before I saw him fumbling to get out of his chair behind the desk. "Wait!" he called out, before grabbing my arm gently. I froze, as I felt electricity surge through me. The same surge I had felt the night that he brought me here when he touched my hands, before grabbing my books. I could feel goosebumps budding from my skin, and I was sure that if he rubbed my arm, he could read it like Braille, and it would tell him how he was making me feel. I *felt* my stomach turning over the same, as it had when I read romance novels, and it was at the climax of the story. I *felt* afraid because he was going to give me back soon, and I was going to get the worst side of Slim and his backwards affection. And I *felt* angry because this wasn't a love story, and he had only captured me to release me.

Khari turned around and glanced at Jahi's hand on my arm, before smacking it away.

"What the fuck you doing, Khari?"

"What does it look like I'm doing? We're going out!" he fussed, as he wildly swept his hand through the air. I didn't even turn my head to watch them argue. I watched through my peripherals, as Khari pushed him into the office and shut the door. Their conversation was muffled, but I could tell that Khari was lighting into him. A few moments later, they emerged from the room, and Jahi leaned against the wall, and I could feel his pensive glare, as he towered over me.

"Have fun, Tove. You look beautiful, and Khari's going to keep you safe."

He wanted me to be safe? And why did I feel like this when he called me beautiful? It had no longer been a compliment but a fact that I knew since I had been told it all of my life.

I had to look at him, but I caught his back, as I saw him sink back into the office, before shutting the door. Slim would've never let me go anywhere so peacefully.

"Let's roll, bitches." Khari gave me a weird smirk, before retrieving his sunglasses from one of the women and sauntering ahead of everyone.

The three women that pampered me got into a van and drove away, as Khari and I got into a red convertible Porsche. Slim had a few nice cars, but nothing like this.

Once in the passenger seat, I let myself melt into the black leather seat, as Khari started to blast rap music, shocking me at his taste, but I didn't question it. I relaxed, as my hair blew in the wind. I would enjoy this while I could.

"This is it!" Khari sang, as we pulled up to a large house that had cars parked outside. You could smell the seafood boil seasoning heavy in the air. Even though Khari had a really nice car, he must've not been worried about it getting taken because he parked on the side of the road like the other cars and left the top down.

After he opened the car door for me, I hesitantly followed behind him, before he suddenly stopped and turned around, before grabbing my hand.

"At the end of the day, I'm a man, and you either walk ahead of me or beside me, but never behind. You are valuable and should be treated, as such." He pulled me along beside him. I didn't know if he was talking about the ransom or what when he called me valuable. "And you have nothing to be nervous about when you're with a Nuru man, so relax."

I nodded, before he pushed open the door so that I could walk into the house first. The house was empty, and everyone seemed to be outback where the loud music was coming from.

As soon as we walked through the sliding door that led to the backyard, a short, full-figured, brown-skinned woman with her hair pulled back into a huge afro puff, ran up to Khari and wrapped her arms around his neck and pulled him into a kiss. They stood there and kissed nastily for about two minutes.

My mouth fell open, as I watched him tongue kiss her while his hands squeezed her ass. When they pulled away from one another, he pointed to me.

"This is Tove. Tove, this is Ashley."

"Hey! Wait, is this her?" she asked Khari, with a finger

pointed to me. He smiled at her and nodded.

"Oh, she *is* gorgeous and *fineee*. Jahi has trouble on his hands," she said, before she pulled me into a hug, making my eyes go big. Why was everyone referencing me to Jahi?

After she pulled away from me, I was led to a table, as Ashley took my hand into hers and Khari followed behind. There had to be about forty people there, and, as we walked through the crowd, all eyes were on us. Every time someone noticed Khari, they either walked up to him and spoke or gave him a respectful head nod. I didn't know what his influence was, but he was definitely respected.

We sat at an empty table, before Ashley ran off to go get us some crawfish, and curiosity got the best of me. I was almost sure that Khari was on the Sweet n' High, but the way he kissed Ashley said differently.

"Is she—is she your girlfriend?" I asked Khari, and he let out a hearty laugh.

"No, indeed. I kiss all of my bitches. Just not you because Jahi would kill me."

"Why would he do that?" I frowned. He looked down at me and took his eyes off of Ashley, before they returned back to her.

"You'll find out."

I shrugged at the cryptic answer, right as Ashley appeared at the table with two trays piled with crawfish, corn, and potatoes. I smiled at the sight. I hadn't had this since I was a little girl and me and my mom would sit on the porch and eat crawfish while she talked shit about the neighbors.

"Thank you." Khari and I simultaneously thanked Ashley.

"Where are you from? That accent is so damned sexy!" Ashley exclaimed, making me chuckle. I could tell that she had a big personality like Khari and was just as loud.

"That's what I'm saying!" Khari laughed.

"Delacroix."

"I love it," she gushed. "You drink?" she practically yelled over the loud music, though it was unnecessary.

"Got any Patrón?" I asked, as her and Khari's necks snapped back in unison.

"Hell fucking yeah! Oh, I like her, Khari!"

"Me too!"

I chuckled, as I watched her take his drink request, before swaying off.

"Sorry we're late. Someone had to get their nails done." A guy and a girl approached the table. You could tell that they were related by their slanted eyes, button noses, and smooth, dark brown complexions. The girl rolled her slanted eyes, before plopping into Khari's lap. I watched in awe, as he kissed her too. Nothing like with Ashley, but *damn*!

The guy must've noticed my expression because he plopped down next to me while chuckling.

"Antony. That's Aniya, my twin." He pointed to the girl in Khari's lap.

"Tove."

"Oh shit, is this her?" The girl broke from her smooches with Khari to look at me in awe. *What had Khari told these people about me?*

"Yup." Khari nodded.

"Oh, I bet Jahi is losing his shit," Antony added.

Before I could respond, Ashley returned with my drink. Everyone watched in awe, as I swallowed the drink in one gulp.

"I love her!" Aniya cheered, making everyone laugh.

The night was so fun, as we ate crawfish until we were stuffed, drank until we were tipsy, and I even danced to Zydeco music —something I hadn't done in forever.

I giggled, as Antony spun me around, before pulling me close. I had learned that this was Khari's tight-knit crew, and everyone was just like him. Loud, rich because of their parents, yet down to earth and fun.

"Your eyes are amazing. I'm a makeup artist, and I'd love for you to model for me," he spoke into my ear, as we swayed from side to side. I took in the dock that was well lit with fairy lights since it was now dark. The environment was so amazing that no one had left yet. Everyone just hung around either talking, drinking, dancing, or all three.

"I don't know about that. I don't think I'm a makeup kind of girl."

"Guurl," he mocked me, before laughing, making me tap his chest. "I understand. But if you ever change your mind..." he trailed off, before shrugging.

"I'll let you know."

I giggled when Khari came behind me, and two-stepped

right along with us, sandwiching me in.

"You ready to go? Mkuu has been worrying me to death for the last hour asking about you," he spoke into my ear, making me turn around in the sandwich to face him; my hands naturally finding their way to his.

"Why is that? Wants to make sure his leverage is safe?" I rose an eyebrow, and that brought that weird, signature grin to Khari's face.

"Mkuu is spoiled. Used to getting what he wants. A little mean and serious, but he's not your enemy. He means you well." I felt Antony kiss my cheek, before leaving Khari and me to sway alone.

"I'm just here for a little while. It doesn't matter what he means. None of this does once I go back. Plus, he's a tyrant."

He chuckled, as he looked down at me.

"He's not so bad." He avoided the conversation about me having to go back. I rested my head against his chest, wrapped my arms around his torso and closed my eyes, as I tried to burn this night into my memory. I wanted to remember the taste of the crawfish, the burn of the Patrón, the way the music thumped from the ground and through my body. I wanted to remember Ashley, Aniya, and Antony. I wanted to remember Khari and the feel of his muscled arms engulfing my frame, as our bodies obeyed the music's rhythm and swayed.

"Let's head out," Khari said, making my eyes open, before I felt him kiss the top of my head. I could've stayed forever. I watched Khari text on his phone, and I wondered if it was

Jahi, but I left that thought alone. I didn't need to be wondering anything about him.

After telling everyone bye and watching Khari tongue down Ashley and Aniya, we were back in the car, but this time we rode in silence, as my hair blew through the wind.

Once we pulled back up to the house that I felt was too large for any one person, I sat there and looked to Khari.

"Thank you." I tried to thank him again, but he shook his head.

"No, thank you."

I wanted to ask him what he was thanking me for, but my door was being pulled open by Jahi. I looked up into his handsome, serious face, and he held out a hand to me. I declined by getting out and walking past him, as I heard Khari chuckle, before lowly telling him to be kind.

I walked up to the door and turned around to wait for him, but he was right there invading my space, as his cologne permeated the air. This was the most dressed down I'd seen him in the black basketball shorts and muscle shirt, as his hair was piled into that loose bun at the top of his head. My breathing hitched in my chest because I didn't expect him to be so close. He stared down into my eyes for a moment, and it almost felt like he was looking through me, like he understood me and my story. But I knew that couldn't be true because our lives were worlds apart.

He reached around me and pushed the door open, before backwards nodding for me to walk in. He wasn't a man of many words like Khari—they were yin and yang.

I turned around and walked through the beautiful house, before I got to the stairs and walked up, feeling his presence close behind.

I fought the urge to look back at him, as I approached the bedroom door. I had nothing to say to him.

I pushed the door open, and when I walked in, I was shocked, and my mouth fell open, before I quickly closed it. There were two bookcases that almost met the ceiling, and they were filled with the books that I brought and many more. I walked up to them and ran my fingers across all of the books' spines, as I read a few titles. All classics mixed in with philosophy, astrology, romance, history and much, much more.

I turned around, and he was leaned against the door frame watching me.

"I didn't know what you liked. But I looked at what you had and got things based off of that. If there's anything else that you want, I can get that for you," he said, as I looked to the bookshelves and to him again. "I wanted to apologize for this morning."

I thought on Barika and Khari's words about him meaning well and being good.

"All is forgiven."

His brows rose slightly from that stoic expression that he usually bore, before he nodded. I grew nervous, as he walked up on me and grabbed my hand, lighting me up with electricity. He gently pulled me to the bathroom that was in the room. He didn't say anything, but I noticed that he had run me a bath with flowers, as the smell of oils filled the bathroom. I looked at our hands, and he pulled his away.

"Barika was sleep, so I ran you a bath. I hope you enjoyed your time with Khari." He turned to me, forcing me to look up at him. My skin ignited, as he brushed a rebel curl from my face from the car ride with Khari. I watched, as his eyes roamed my head, and he nodded his appreciation.

"I like it."

"Thank you."

And just like that, he had left me standing in the bathroom confused. *Why were they being so nice to me and doing all of this? Was this some sick joke? And why did his touch feel like that?* I mentally cursed myself for allowing that feeling back into my chest, though I seemed to have little control over it. I stood there for a moment longer, before shedding my clothes and submerging my body into the warm water and allowing the combined scent of the flowers and oils to tickle my nose and relax me. I was going to have to snap myself out of this and not let them break my barrier with this weird kindness. I thought that being taken for ransom was supposed to be torture, but this was... this was something else.

After drying off, I slipped on some of the silk pajamas that Khari brought me, before I snuggled under the covers and stared toward the ceiling. I tried to fight the smile that spread across my lips at the fact that I didn't have to try to imagine the popcorn ceilings tonight, but it was to no avail. My heavy lids and the thoughts of the day drifted me to sleep.

Chapter Seven

JAHI

I was awakened from my sleep by the sound of my phone on the nightstand. I groaned because on Saturdays, I typically slept in a little later and enjoyed not having Djimon around.

I felt around for the phone with my eyes closed, and once I grabbed it, I instinctively navigated the answer button.

"Hello?"

"Heyyyyy, baby bro! Were you sleeping? It doesn't matter. Anyway!"

"Khari, what the fuck do you want? It's—" I pulled the phone away from my face to glance at the time with one eye open.

"It's eleven o'clock, nigga! Wake yo' ass up!"

I huffed, before sitting up in bed. Khari was not going to

stop calling. And if I ignored him or hung up on him, he would pop up at my house.

"So, I went out of town to go party, but I called to make sure that you did something with Tove today. Take her to lunch, see if she wants to see a movie. Something," he ranted. I laid back down, as soon as he said that he was out of town.

"Uh, Khari I don't know if you've noticed, but her ass don't like me. I put those bookshelves in her room and found all of those books, and I didn't even get so much as a thank you. She just told me that all was forgiven for that morning."

"Well, you were being an ass. Also, she is a woman that you are interested in, not your prisoner, and not one of those hoes that you fuck. So, take her out of the damn house! She might just surprise you. Oh, and Mkuu, tell her yo' name!"

"What?" I frowned.

"She's been staying in that house with you for four days, and you never told her your name, asshole."

I frowned and realized that he was right. But she wouldn't talk to me, so how was I supposed to introduce myself? "Alright, but surprise me how? And I called yo' ass all night to get the details on how shit went and to see what you learned about her."

"And I texted and told you that everything was fine and that you would have to find out things about her on your own," he stated, matter-of-factly.

I was getting frustrated with this shit. I never had to ask a woman out or ask for anything. I spoke, and people listened to me.

"Take her where, Khari? I—I, never been on no date before," I grumbled.

"Aww, that's so cute, butttt that's your job to find that out. See what she likes. Now. Ta-ta! I got meats to see and niggas to meet!"

I grimaced. Before I could respond, he hung up. He was always taking shit too far. After getting up, brushing my teeth, and showering, I went into my closet and placated on what to wear. Shit, I didn't even know where to take her.

After settling on something casual, I put on a white button-up, tailored olive pants and camel Diego low top sneakers. They were the least expensive shoes that I had, but I liked them.

After putting on my watch, I left out of my room and stepped into the hallway. Although Tove's room was right across from mine, there was a lot of distance between ours. I had given her the room that my parents usually occupied if they stayed over after a celebration.

I was shocked to see her door cracked open. She usually kept it like Fort Knox. Curiosity got the best of me, and I eased the door open further. I wondered what she did when no one was looking. *Did she just sit there and stare and read in-between?* But when I cracked the door open, I was surprised to see her making the bed with Barika. She still had on her silky pajamas, so she must've slept in late too.

I watched, as they moved in unison and silence. Maybe this was another reason Barika liked her so much. I felt a tinge of disappointment in myself for never thinking to help

Barika out. I planned on getting more staff when I started a family—a butler, nanny, another maid, groundkeepers and all, but I had never personally thought to help her. She cleaned this whole house by herself and never really complained.

It wasn't until they finished and Barika looked up at me, did Tove turn around and give me her attention. She looked at me, expectantly, waiting to see what I wanted.

"Uh," I cleared my throat. "I was wondering if you wanted to go to lunch with me?" I felt corny for even asking. The shit was weird.

I watched, as she looked from the bookshelves, then to the floor. I was about to tell her ass never mind and retreat because I was feeling played already, until she looked up and nodded her head.

"Cool. Just let me know when you're ready. I'll be in my office," I told her, causing her eyebrows to dip, as she looked me up and down.

"Uh, what do I wear?" she spoke with every word drawled out.

"Whatever you want to wear." I shrugged, and she nodded, before turning to face a smiling Barika. Barika never smiled at my ass. I went to my office, and again it felt like forever when I was waiting on her. It was like father time worked for Tove.

I was about to go check on her and see if she changed her mind, when she appeared in the doorway of my office. My eyes traveled from her feet on up, as I took in her wearing tan colored shoes and a white t-shirt dress. Her face glowed, as it was surrounded by her mass of dark wavy curls.

"Sorry I took so long. I had a lot of stuff to sort through." I closed my eyes briefly, as she spoke. Her voice elicited an array of feelings. Her voice felt like a cool breeze on a warm summer night or iced cold water that quenched your thirst on a sweltering hot day. It pulled you in like a siren's song.

"It's fine," I told her, as I got up and approached her. I pushed back a curl that had fallen into her face, and I felt her tense up. She froze every time that I touched her, and I didn't know if that was good or bad, but I felt compelled to touch her the few times that I could. "Ready?"

She nodded.

"What would you like to eat?" I asked her once we were in the car, making her mouth open then close again, before she looked toward me.

"I don't know. I'm not picky." She shrugged, and I nodded. This shit was awkward. I had never been out on a date, but I knew when I took my mama to lunch, she always had a ton of her own ideas and things that she had a taste for.

"So, I see that Barika really likes you." I tried to start a conversation, and that brought a small grin to her lips, but it didn't really meet her eyes.

"Yeah, I guess she does."

"She was a gift from my grandparents."

I didn't have to turn my head to know that she was giving me that glare. I felt her pensively glaring at my profile.

"Gift? So, people are things to acquire to you? Like a

painting or a car?" she asked flatly but voice still filled with sultriness.

"Nah. I wasn't saying it like that. I was just saying that my grandparents brought her for... like she works for me because they brought her to the states and—"

"Like the Transatlantic slave trade?" she cut in.

"No. Like they got her a green card to come work for us in the states."

"Hmm," she hummed.

I decided to just cut the radio up and be quiet until we got to the restaurant, since trying to talk to her wasn't making the situation any better.

———

Menu. Eyes. Menu. Eyes.

My eyes kept going from the menu to her dead-like gaze. I had decided on Fleming's since I had a taste for steak, and she hadn't offered any suggestions.

I sat there thinking about the many ways that I could kill Khari. I should've just left her alone and let her do her thing at the house or offered for Craig to take her wherever she wanted to go. But Khari was right, she *wasn't* my prisoner, and I did want to know more about her.

"Any idea on what you want to get?" I tried to talk to her again, and that briefly broke her gaze, as she brought her eyes to her menu, before they returned to mine. She looked... *nervous*, as she sighed.

"Not exactly. Everything here is so expensive."

"Not real—" I caught myself, as she raised an eyebrow. "Uh, they have the best steak. Do you eat red meat?"

She nodded. "But I've never had steak. What does it taste like?"

I was surprised that she was actually giving me conversation.

I chuckled because I had never been asked that, and the flavor of steak was a hard thing to describe. "It's one of those things you'd just have to try. It's not really relatable to chicken or ground beef or anything like that."

She nodded, before glancing back at the menu. She had finally settled on the crab cakes, and I got the steak, and the table fell back into an uncomfortable silence. This dating shit was corny, as fuck.

"My name is Jahi Ife Nuru, but my family calls me Mkuu."

Her eyebrows knitted together.

"My name, I never told you my name."

Her face lit with recognition of what I was talking about. "Oh, what does Mkuu mean?"

"Prince."

"Fitting." She mocked surprise with her eyebrows briefly rising to her hairline.

"What's your whole name? Any nicknames?" I asked, as she bore a strange expression.

"Tove Monroe. No, no nicknames."

"No middle name?"

"No. My ma said that two names were more than enough to last you a lifetime."

I nodded at the odd saying. In my culture, you could have several.

"Where you from?"

"The bayou. Why does everyone keep asking me that?" she drawled.

I tapped my lips, and she gave a curt nod, before I asked, "Where are your parents?"

"Dead," she said it so flat, like it meant nothing to her.

"I'm sorry."

"Circle of life." She shrugged. "What about you?"

"They're around, and loud."

She chuckled. Hearing her laugh oddly had me on edge.

"I reckon that's where Khari gets it from."

I nodded.

"You had fun with Khari?"

"The best I've had in a long time." She grinned, and this time it met her sparkling eyes. I felt a little jealous that I wasn't able to make her smile like that.

"That's good. He has that way with people."

"Why did you buy me those bookshelves if I'm only staying until Slim gets you the money?"

I wanted to tell her that Slim was never getting her back and that he had run off, but I didn't want her to try and run off too just yet.

"Built," I corrected.

"What?"

"You asked why I bought you those bookshelves, but I built them. I started on them the night that you came. Carpentry is a hobby that Khari and I were taught at a young age." She just stared at me, so I continued with my questioning. "I can't treat you with respect and keep you comfortable?"

"No one has ever cared to do so before." I noticed that even when she spoke of negative things, her voice remained flat and her face remained expressionless, like it didn't bother her.

I wanted to ask her more, but we were interrupted by our food being brought to the table. A silence fell amongst us again, but this time it was comfortable. I just figured that maybe we both were naturally quiet people.

I prayed over my food, and although she didn't bow her head, she still waited for me to eat. I wanted to ask her more about her beliefs, but I saw how that ended last time and decided against it.

I watched, as her low eyes kept glancing at my steak.

"You want to try it?" I offered, making her low eyes flow to my face. I never shared or anything like that, but with her, I wanted to. I wanted to share my living space with her, my food, and even my free time.

"Can I?" she asked, surprising me. Everything had felt so forced a moment ago. Maybe we both weren't used to this. Which was odd if she worked for Slim and had been around men all the time to make a living.

"Yes." I sliced her a piece of the medium cooked steak,

and when I looked up, she held her mouth open so that I could feed it to her. I placed the steak into her mouth, and a little juice from the steak dripped from her full bottom lip, and I caught it with my thumb. It was odd because it seemed that suddenly, we were comfortable with one another.

I brought my thumb to my lips and licked the juice off, as she watched me tentatively.

"It's good," she said, as she stared at my lips and chewed.

"Yeah?"

"Mhm." She nodded, before swallowing. "I wish I would've gotten that."

"Want some?" She pointed to her crab cakes, and though I didn't care for them, I didn't want to decline any interaction with her, so I nodded. I felt like a feen for her attention, and that shit was lame to me.

She picked up her fork and brought it to my lips the same as I had done her, and I accepted.

"Mkuu!" I heard my father's thunderous voice.

I watched, as her low eyes widened, making her lids disappear like an anime character.

I turned my head to see my parents, and I didn't miss the look of disgust on my mother's face. I guess they saw her feeding me. I didn't want her to meet them right now because they could be a lot to take in.

"Baba, what are you two doing here?" I questioned, as my father welcomed himself to our table, pulling a chair out for my mother.

"Djimon didn't tell you that we were supposed to have

lunch today? You were supposed to meet us an hour ago, but when you didn't show, we called him, and he told us where you were." I had forgotten all about the lunch, and I made a mental note to stop sharing my location with Djimon on my phone—after I beat his ass.

"My bad. I forgot. Baba, mama, this is Tove. Tove, these are my parents, Mr. and Mrs. Nuru."

My father's eyes lit with recognition, as he cut his eyes toward me, before smiling at Tove. He knew all about us taking her from Slim. What he didn't know was the real reason why. We had told him a different deadline and price than the one we gave Slim, so he wouldn't grow suspicious.

"Nice to meet you, Tove," my father greeted, as he took her hand and kissed it. Even when displeased, he was always polite.

"Likewise. It's nice to meet you, as well, Mrs. Nuru," I was relieved that she spoke. For a second, I was worried that she would go back mute. Khari was right about her surprising me.

I felt my eyebrow tent, when my mother declined to speak to her.

"Mama, this is Tove," I repeated.

"I hear you," she said smugly. I could tell that she was pissed because her accent was thick as hell at the moment. I glanced at Tove, and her head was down, as she focused on her food. I could somehow feel her shutting back down.

"So, what are you two having? Is it too late for us to join you?" my father asked, trying to break the tension, as he was already calling the waitress over for a menu.

"Well, wouldn't it be polite if you spoke to her?" I persisted.

"I don't speak to whores," she scoffed.

"Hediye!" my father immediately scolded her.

"Excuse me." Tove hopped up from her seat, smoothed her hands down the front of her dress, and darted off.

"Really, mama?"

"What?" She feigned innocence. "That is not your wife, and I don't know why you would bring her on a date." Her accent was getting thicker, if that shit was even possible.

"It's not a date. It's lunch."

"How is it not a date when you two were feeding one another? Why waste your time with women that you have no future with?"

"Mkuu!" my father bellowed, as I got up and reached into my pocket and pulled out enough bills to cover my food and theirs. I wasn't going to disrespect my mother and argue with her, but I wasn't going to let her mistreat Tove either. I brought her into my life, so I had to protect her and make sure that she wasn't being mistreated, even by my own mother and her bullshit. On top of that, her ass was fucking up my progress.

"Look, baba. I have to go." I gave him a hug and kissed my mother's cheek. She didn't say a word or reciprocate the kiss.

"Mkuu," he tried again, following me out of the private dining area of the restaurant. I knew Tove was outside because she didn't walk to the bathroom reserved for this area.

"Yeah, baba?" I blew out a frustrated breath, halting in my stride once we were standing outside of the restaurant.

"Why are you behaving this way? Your mother may have said it the wrong way, but she wasn't lying. She is not your wife. Do we need to place her elsewhere until her ransom is met? I saw the way that you were looking at her."

I frowned at the thought of sending Tove somewhere else.

"She's mine. She ain't going nowhere."

"Mkuu, are you falling for her? It is a prostitute's way to charm men. And she is not yours. Your wife, the woman you will marry and have children with, is in Tanzania. I know she looks pretty, but all that you can offer her is sex, nothing more. And Nuru men don't fuck prostitutes."

My gaze fell to Tove, who was leaned against my car, as she watched cars pass by. I knew what I was obligated to do, and up until I saw her, I didn't give a fuck. That prostitute thing bothered me, but not nearly as much as the urge to get to know her.

"I hope that you and mama enjoy your lunch." I patted my father's shoulder, before walking away from him. He called my name a few times, but I just continued to walk away. This was an argument that I didn't want to have. I was still trying to sort through what I was feeling for Tove and why I was so drawn to her.

"I'm sorry about my parents," I apologized, as I walked up to Tove, but she kept her eyes ahead. That shit irked me because apologizing wasn't my thing, yet I had done so with her twice.

I could tell by the dead look in her eyes that she had shut down again. I blew out a frustrated breath, feeling defeated and back to step one with her. I rounded the car to open the door for her, and she didn't look at me, as she got in.

Once we got back to the house, she quickly got out of the car and waited by the door for me.

"Tove," I called her name once I opened the door, in an attempt to talk to her again, but she rushed up the stairs. It took everything in me not to bark a command at her. Nobody ever disrespected me the way she had.

But I knew that would just make the shit worse. I called Khari, and he didn't answer the damn phone. I sat around for a few moments to see if she would leave the room, but she never did. This shit with her wasn't working. I may have to let her go.

———

A week later...

I found myself in the VIP section of one of the strip clubs that I frequented from time to time. I had come with Deon, but he went to get a private dance, which meant he went to go fuck. We had just left a meeting, and it turned out that my takeover of the East was a good idea. There were several untapped illegal businesses that had risen in the area since we last visited the idea of taking over.

"What's wrong?" the stripper named Lotus asked, as she

swayed to the music and danced in my lap. I placed a few hundred in her thong.

"Nothing," I lied. I had been trying to talk to Tove for a week now, and I got nothing in return.

"I know you better than that, Jahi."

I looked up into her pretty dark brown face, before my eyes fell down to her body. She was stacked, as fuck.

"Then you should know I'on like to talk."

She chuckled, before taking a seat in my lap and turning sideways to face me.

"Jahi, what's wrong?" she persisted. On a very rare occasion, I'd talk to her. She had a weird ass way of pulling it out of you.

I glared at her, but she didn't budge.

"A woman—"

"Oh my gosh there's a woman?" she gushed, making me shove at her to push her ass out of my lap.

"Wait! No, I'm just surprised! Tell me about her. Is she pretty?" she asked, as she wrapped her arms around my neck, trying to hold on, before I let her be.

I nodded.

"Prettier than me?" She pointed a long fingernail toward herself.

I smirked then nodded. She didn't take offense to it. She knew how I was.

"What's going on? I've never seen you stressed behind a woman."

"She's an asshole." I took a sip of my water. I didn't drink alcohol.

"Oh well, you've found your wife. If any woman can have you in your feelings and calling her an asshole, then I would say you've met your match." She smirked.

"Wouldn't know. She won't talk to me."

"Oh, you're just in hell, aren't you? A woman that isn't wooed by your presence alone?"

"Fuck you." I chuckled, as she did the same.

"I'm just saying. Maybe you aren't putting in enough effort. Shit, maybe she been through some shit with men. I know I have." She shrugged. "If you think she's worth it, then try harder and think outside of yourself and what you want. Try to find out what she wants. You're spoiled, Jahi. Used to getting everything and anyone that you want, so you've never been challenged. I just know you aren't giving it your all," she concluded, before getting up from my lap and leaving the section. She always did that shit. Said some shit to make you think and then left. Before I could think about what Tove could've been through, a tall, light-skinned chick with a slim thick body came to the entrance of my section. She had some weird, dark eyes that made me feel like I might've seen her ass before, but with me, there wasn't no telling. I nodded my head at Craig to let her in. I needed to fuck, and though she wasn't what I wanted, she would suffice.

"I'm Noelle," she introduced herself over the music. I glanced at her from head to toe and nodded appreciatively at how she filled out the pink mini dress.

"I don't care."

She laughed, but it wasn't a joke. I wouldn't remember her name anyway.

"Jahi, right?" she asked, as she took a seat next to me. She knew who I was, and I wasn't a conversationalist. I got up from my seat and headed toward the exit, and once I got outside, I looked over my shoulder and just as suspected, she had followed me. Deon could catch a fucking Uber or some shit.

Once in the back of my car, she immediately dropped to her knees, as Craig drove to my house. I only really used his services for meetings and family gatherings. Any other time, I drove and protected myself. My family disapproved, but nobody was gon' fuck with me. They either knew better or became an example.

"Ouch!" she yelped when I snatched her head back by her hair. She was trying to suck my dick raw, and I ain't play that. I pulled a condom from my pocket, and she got the message. I laid my head back, as she topped me off on the way to my house, but I couldn't get into it.

I wanted to tell Craig to take her ass somewhere else but decided against it because I needed to bust a nut.

I expected Barika to be sleep and Tove to have her door locked, as I walked upstairs with what's her name.

"This is nice!" she blurted, causing me to look down and scowl at her loud ass while I lifted a hand like I was about to bop her ass in the mouth.

"Sorry," she mumbled and ducked.

Once we got upstairs, I was shocked that Tove had her door wide open.

"Who is that?" the girl asked, but I quickly shoved her into my room, before she even finished the question, and Tove slowly turned her head in my direction. I stared at her for a moment, before she turned her head back toward the TV and picked up the Sprite bottle from her nightstand, where I noticed some Tums sitting. I didn't even know she watched TV or did anything besides reading and staring.

Her hair was pulled in a wild ponytail at the top of her head, and she looked a little flushed like she didn't feel good. Her mean ass saw me still staring at her and got up to slam the door.

I felt weird, like I had got caught cheating or some shit. When I went into my bedroom, the chick was already on top of my bed naked.

"Who was that? Your sister?" She pointed at the door.

"Turn around," I instructed, as she smiled at me, before doing so and put her ass in the air. I reached into my pocket, before I sheathed my dick and walked up to her, spread her cheeks and dipped in. I was about to catch my nut then get rid of her question asking ass.

"Mmm, baby," she moaned, as I started to pound at her dripping wet center. Her shit was actually decent; way better than her head. "Fuck, wait, that's my spot!" She tried to reach back, but I pushed her hand away, before reaching around to grab her breasts and continuing to drill into her. After two more strokes, she was trembling, and a while later, I was filling the condom up. It took longer than I wanted to since she was doing all that yelling and shit.

Once I pulled away from her, she fell against the bed, before turning around. "That was so good. Those rumors were true, as fuck." Her chest heaved up and down.

I chuckled at that. "You can give the driver your address, and he'll take you wherever you need to go." I walked into the bathroom and flushed the condom and turned around to find her in the doorway.

"What? No round two or nothing? I can't even stay the night?" Her face was drenched in hurt.

"You need help finding your way out?" I asked, as I cut the shower on, before returning my gaze to her.

"Nigga, fuck you. Your dick wasn't all that anyway. Shit was quick, as fuck," she spat, with her cute face balled up, before marching off. I watched as she got dressed, before I stepped into the shower. Weird ass bitch didn't have to pee after she had sex or nothing.

I took a long, hot shower and contemplated on what Lotus said and how Khari was always telling my ass to be kind and treat Tove better than I treated other women. Once I stepped out of the shower, all remnants of the girl were gone, including her name from my mind.

After drying off and throwing on some deodorant and boxers, I opened my door to see if Tove's was still shut and it was. I was tired of her ignoring me in my own damn house and treating me like a bitch, so I opened the door to her bedroom, and the TV was turned off. She laid with her back to the door.

"Get out," she drawled lowly. She definitely wasn't feeling good.

"You're not feeling well?" I asked, but she ignored me. I was over that shit, so I pulled back the covers and got in behind her ass. I felt her tense when I pulled her into me, before she relaxed against my chest. "What's wrong, Tove?"

"My stomach hurts. Now get out." I ignored her, as I brought my hand to her flat stomach and started rubbing it.

"You need anything?"

"No, Barika got me some Tums, so I been eating those for the past three days."

I frowned and lifted my head a little. "You've been sick all this time and ain't tell me nothing?"

"Why would you care? I'm just a whore that's here for ransom money. Leave me alone and go call someone else over, Jahi." I wanted to laugh at how weird my name sounded coming from her mouth.

I brought her little thick ass closer. I had never done this before, but it was comfortable, as fuck. She was telling me to leave her alone like I didn't notice her snuggle into the arm I had placed under her head.

"I'll take you to my family's doctor in the morning."

"No, just leave me alone. I'll be alright."

I ignored her, as I continued to rub her stomach. I couldn't leave her alone if I wanted to, and this past week, I had been trying hard to convince myself to. I was trying to tell myself to let her go and that maybe she missed her old life, but I didn't care, and if that made me selfish then, oh well.

We exchanged no words, as I laid with her and rubbed her stomach until I heard her breathing heavily. I wasn't going to let her sleep alone, knowing that she wasn't feeling well and hadn't been for three days. Shit, when Khari or I wasn't feeling well, we stayed by our parents, and our mama made us all kind of soup, tea, and remedies.

Why did I care about her ass when she didn't want to be cared for? Or was that shit just a front because she had been through some shit like Lotus said? I didn't know because she was a brick wall, but that was okay because I was persistent when I wanted something. I had never wanted anything more than to know her; everything and everyone else was easy.

Chapter Eight

TOVE

M y heavy eyes fluttered open, and the first sense that was triggered was my sense of smell, then came touch. I immediately smelled his body wash surrounding me, and then I realized that he still had a hand on my stomach and his bare chest against my back. I didn't want to let him hold me, but it felt so good. I felt so safe when he held me, and in that moment, I really needed that.

I had been feeling like shit for days now, and I didn't know if it was because I ate richer foods here or what. Slim had me on a strict diet because he didn't want me to gain too much weight, but Jahi didn't give a damn. He had Barika feeding my ass all kinds of stuff.

I slowly turned around to face him to avoid waking him

up, but I noticed that he was already awake. He was just looking back at me with low eyes.

"You feeling any better?" he asked, as he touched my stomach, before pulling me back into him. I didn't resist him. I *couldn't*.

I shook my head.

"Okay. I made an appointment for nine, so you should go shower and get yourself together."

Why did he care how I felt? The lunch, the bookshelves, Khari, this all was just confusing to me. I had already been trying to avoid him since lunch. I had heard what his father said about his arranged marriage.

I was getting beside myself, but his mother's words put me right back in my place. I wasn't a whore, but I didn't belong to him, and I needed that reminder to not get attached.

"Okay," I told him, as he watched me get up from the bed and go to the bathroom. I took a hot shower after brushing my teeth and flossing. On my way out of the bathroom, I gripped my stomach. My stomach had been really upset, and those Tums and Sprite weren't working. I walked out of the bathroom in my bath towel to find Jahi finishing up on changing my sheets.

"Where's Barika?" My eyebrows dipped.

"I gave her the day off." He shrugged. I was surprised being that she had worked every day since I had been here. His eyes ran amuck over my body once I dropped my towel. Usually, nudity meant nothing to me, but watching him watch me made me nervous, so I quickly dipped into the closet.

I was trying to reach for the folded t-shirts on the top shelf, before I felt his muscular bare chest against my back.

He grabbed one of the shirts for me, and I turned around and looked up into his face. His eyes were filled with lust, and I was sure that mine were the same, as I looked up into his handsome face. Jahi was introducing me to all kinds of feelings. Feelings that I had only read about. He leaned down to kiss me, and I stood on the tips of my toes in an attempt to meet him halfway. My eyes fluttered closed, as he kissed me deeply, before pulling away. My body felt charged with electricity, and the Braille covered my arms.

I watched with lowered lids, as he walked over to the bench that was in the middle of the closet, next to the display that held all of the jewelry that Khari bought for me. He beckoned me over with a wave of his hand, and I obeyed.

"Hh!" I gasped when he wrapped his arms around my waist and latched onto one of my breasts and suckled on my nipple. I gripped his head, as one of his hands found my center, and he began to toy with my clit. I couldn't help the moans that came from my mouth and echoed off the walls of the closet.

Right when I felt the pressure building in my stomach, he had taken his hand away, before placing my leg over his shoulder and replacing his hand with his mouth.

"Shittt," I hissed. This was nothing like what I experienced before. I actually wanted this, and it was nothing but pure pleasure. My heart raced, as I felt his lips wrap around my clit, and he sucked on it, stiffening his tongue against it, as he brought his hand back and slid his fingers inside of me. Shortly after, I was trembling, as my eyes watered and my hips bucked forward while intoxication took over, and I was on a high. I couldn't stop myself from calling out in pleasure, as my eyes roamed to watch him with his eyes closed in delight, as he feasted on me. I didn't want to, in fear of messing up his rhythm, but I placed my hands on his head for balance. It didn't matter, because he licked and sucked and repeated until I was done trembling and then he did it all over again until I was trembling to the point where I could barely stand on that one leg anymore. He let my leg down and held me up, before standing and staring down at me. He wiped at his face with the back of his hand, where my juices drenched all the way down into his beard.

I felt weird, like I had just connected to him. Like we had just had a deep conversation, and I had laid myself bare. It was like we had just established a sexual dialect that only we knew, which was weird because most times, I felt as if I couldn't stand him.

"Go get dressed," he tapped my thigh, but I wasn't ready for that yet. I felt like I wanted to speak more of this language, after all, he was the only one who knew it. Before he could walk away, I reached into his shorts and pulled out his thick, long dick, as it responded to my touch. After seeing the size, I wanted to renege, but it was too late because he had already lifted me into his arms and started to kiss me, as his thick head prodded at my entrance.

"Hhhh!" I gasped against his lips, as he started to make his way inside of me. My arms were locked around his neck, as I breathed into his mouth while he lifted me up and down his length.

"Mmm!" I moaned loudly, as my head fell back in sensual gratification. He attacked my neck with his lips, as he groaned and moaned loudly against it. Those tears came to my eyes again, but I rolled my eyes to deter them. I dropped my head forward, and we became forehead to forehead, staring into one another's eyes when my body started to shake uncontrollably out of sync with my erratic moans and his well-paced groans that forced themselves out of his throat every time that he sunk into me.

"*Wewe ni wangu,*" he muttered against my lips causing my eyebrows to dip in confusion, before my head fell back again, a reflex to a new set of tremors. He was an 8.9 earthquake named Jahi, and he was disturbing and erupting everything within me. Each thrust and act of kindness or affection, chiseled at my fortress of mental protection.

I watched his eyes close taut, as his strokes slowed, but thrusts stayed strong, before I felt him twitching inside of me with my walls tightening around him, as we both moaned and came together. He stood there with my legs still in the crooks of his arms, drenched in sweat and nothing left to say, as if we had just said it all.

"I'm sorry. I know you don't feel well. I just got distracted and—"

He tried to apologize, but I just shook my head. I felt like my soul needed that. I had just *given* myself to someone for the first time, and I was okay with that. It was a pure act of free will.

We said nothing, as he carried me to the en-suite bathroom, before cutting the shower on. I was learning that in a world where everyone was always talking at me, he and I didn't need many words. We were quiet, as we washed one another in the shower, and we were quiet, as we parted ways to get dressed. Even the ride to the doctor was quiet with him only questioning how I felt. My thoughts started to flip around in my mind like a Rubik's cube, as I contemplated how Slim was going to kill me if he found out that I had given myself to someone and that I enjoyed it—unlike what he forced upon me. As if he knew my thoughts, Jahi grabbed my hand, before pulling it to his lips and kissing the back of it, and that was enough to put me at ease for the moment and that moment only.

———

"Ms. Monroe, did you hear me?" Jahi's family's doctor, Dr. Laissez, asked. I just stared at her for a while, before I nodded. "Well, I'm going to leave and let you get dressed, and I'll go give Jahi an update."

I grabbed her arm, startling her, before she could walk away.

"Let me tell him, please," I pleaded with her, as I felt my eyes glaze over. She hesitated.

"I'm supposed to report back to him."

"I promise I'll tell him. Please, just let me do it." My voice trembled, and that was unrecognizable to me.

She looked me over a second longer, before plastering a warm smile on her face and saying, "Okay."

I quickly got dressed and ripped up the ultrasound papers, before throwing them in the trash can. I was stupid to ever think that I could enjoy something. Stupid to even entertain the thought of getting away scot-free from Slim. Not only had he taken years of my life, but his child was also now nestled in my womb. My life was riddled with disappointment and disaster, as if those two words should've been my middle names.

I walked out of the doctor's office, and Jahi looked up at me expectantly, before standing up.

"It's some digestion issues from eating different foods," I lied.

"That's what she said?" He looked confused, and I felt caught but nodded my head anyway.

"I just have to give my body time to adjust and keep it light for now."

"Okay. And that's it? She didn't come and tell me anything." He raised an eyebrow.

"I told her that I would tell you since it wasn't anything major."

"Okay." He looked at me a moment longer, before saying, "I want to take you somewhere." It was my turn to look confused, but he just grabbed my hand and pulled me along with him out of the doctor's office.

Once we were in the car, I mulled over my thoughts, before looking over at his handsome, stern face, as he focused on the road.

"Can I ask you a question?" I queried.

"Mhm."

"Where is Slim? It's been weeks, and he was supposed to have that money to you the next day, right?" I needed confirmation on something.

I watched, as his jaw tightened.

"What? You in a fucking rush to get back to that nigga or something?" he practically growled.

"No."

"Then what the fuck you asking me that shit for?"

"Because I should know where I'll be and when I'll be returning."

"You ain't ever going back. That nigga that you rushing to ran off and he never came up with the money."

That just didn't sound like Slim to give up so easily. *And why was he keeping me if he no longer needed me?*

"Well, why am I still with you then?" I asked lowly.

"Because I want you to be. You wanna leave?" He glanced from the road to me.

"Do I have a choice?" I asked because I was sure that he wouldn't want anything to do with me after this news. And if I could leave, before being rejected, then I would. My life was painful enough.

"Fuck no."

"Jahi..."

"Fuck no!" he barked. "Yo' ass ain't going nowhere."

"I'm not an object. I'm a person," I objected solemnly.

"My person," he mumbled. When Slim would stake claim on me, I wanted to crawl out of my skin and die, but in this car right here with 8.9 Jahi, I was suffocating with that indescribable feeling in my chest, as I bit back tears because for some reason, I wanted nothing more than to be *his person*. The electricity that he caused to make my skin form Braille was unexplainable, and the shit was crazy because I hardly even knew him. We had worlds between us that would never collide, and he was set to marry someone else. This was Romeo and Juliet territory. We were doomed if we ever tried to make anything out of this.

I sat quietly in the passenger seat and wondered how I had even gotten pregnant. I had never been pregnant before, and after reading so many books, I chalked it up to me being aggressively raped my second night there, as a gun was pressed to my temple while Slim barked out commands.

I thought back to the night that I thought me and Lani could be friends. I remembered laying in the bed in my own blood that seeped from between my legs, before she stood over me and sighed. Her eyes looked like she felt my pain. I remembered her helping me into the tub and washing my back, as I sobbed and held my legs. She had cleaned me up and put fresh sheets on the bed and rubbed my back. I didn't know that she wasn't really there for me until she leaned to my ear and whispered, "Better you than me," before she pulled back and gave me a sly grin. I wasn't shocked. After all, my own father had just sold me, but I was disappointed. That's why I never understood why she hated me so much. I replaced her, and she got to get away from him but decided to stick around. Maybe she had Stockholm's syndrome. Maybe we all did since he had acquired most of us in similar ways. I remember the day when Slim decided that he no longer needed to secretly jab a gun in my back while taking me in public. He said that it took longer with me than most, but he was still successful in breaking me.

When we pulled up to the bookstore where I first saw him, I narrowed my eyes at him. He didn't say anything, as he opened the door for me, and I slowly got out. I cautiously followed him inside, as he unlocked the door, and I just stood there and marveled at the revamped bookstore. There was nothing but bookshelves like the ones in the bedroom that I occupied and aisles and aisles of books. Even the café had been renovated and had new white and gold marble countertops.

I turned around to look at him, as he stood by the door with a menacing glare on his face. He was obviously still upset from our conversation in the car.

"What are we doing here?"

"Well, Barika told me that you read everything at home. And I know you don't want to be trapped in the house all day, so I bought you this store. You'll get new books all the time, you'll make your own money, and you can get out and get fresh air. I don't want you to feel like a prisoner to my home.

If there's anything that you want to change, then we can. The old employees would like to still work here, if that's okay with you, or we can hire new ones. It's all at your discretion."

I quickly turned my back to him and rolled my eyes upward to divert the tears. I briefly thought back to a book that I read about love languages and realized that if Jahi was exhibiting his love languages, then one of his most prominent love languages was acts of service.

I couldn't help myself, as I ran into him, wrapped my arms around him and buried my face into his chest in hopes that the fabric of his shirt would prevent me from crying. Something I hadn't done in years—and so far, hugging him worked. I wanted to cry so bad because someone had finally paid attention to me and heard my cry for help without me even speaking to him, but I couldn't keep him. I couldn't keep any of this.

"Thank you," I let out through shaky breaths. He engulfed me in his arms, before pulling my head up by my chin and kissing my lips with his supple ones.

"You don't have to thank me; I'll do anything for you except let you go," he spoke seriously. It was like he could read my mind.

I just nodded my head because I didn't want him to start yelling again. It was pointless.

Once we got back to the house, he told me that he had to go handle some business, and just like that, he was gone. I guessed Barika took advantage of her day off because she was gone, as well. I stripped out of my clothes and sat in the middle of the bed, bringing my knees to my chest, as I just let go. I bawled until my eyes were sore, and so was my throat. I called out to my ma, as if she could hear me because I needed some type of saving grace. I had never been a needy person, but I needed mercy just this once.

Chapter Nine

TOVE

"Favorite color?"

"Blue. You?" I asked, as I sat with my legs crossed on the countertop of the bookstore while reading a magazine, as Jahi stood behind me with his arms wrapped around my waist. It had been a week since he gifted me the store, and we were waiting on the sign to be changed to *Cover Cove* and for a few more books, before we opened it back up. I asked to come here to read the books and magazines we had since I had read all of the ones at the house.

We had been getting to know each other slowly, since he was busy a lot with working, and I was trying to not divulge too much of myself, since things between us wouldn't last anyway. It was pointless to get too deep in, so it was helpful that he was gone a lot.

"Green."

I felt my face ball up. I never liked the color.

"What you frowning for? You have green eyes." He chuckled.

"And they've always gotten me in trouble."

"What do you mean?"

"More attention. More trouble."

"I can attest to that." He kissed my neck.

"You drink? I never see you drink anything but water. Not even a sip of juice."

"I don't. Water is all that I ever drink, do you?"

"I'd drink liquor like a fish drinks water if I could."

"That's some bayou shit. What you like? Moonshine?"

I looked at him over my shoulder, as he flashed me that pretty smile that was similar to Khari's but unique in its own way.

"Wowww. Isn't that racist or some shit?"

He started to laugh, making me laugh in turn.

"I don't think that's how racism works. It is stereotyping though," he acknowledged.

"Well, I like Patrón, hold the moonshine, please. Do you smoke weed?"

"Nope. Do you?"

"Nah. But aren't you African?" I jabbed.

"Isn't that racist or some shit?"

"Nah, that's stereotyping though." We started laughing, until I snorted and slapped my hand over my mouth.

"What the fuck was that?" he laughed harder, as he nuzzled my neck, making me squirm because I was ticklish.

"I haven't done that in years. That's so embarrassing." I buried my face into my magazine, before he snatched it away, forcing me to look at him.

"I like it."

"Hmm, is that right?" I asked, as he leaned in for a kiss. We hadn't had sex since the first time, but we kissed a lot. It was a good thing that we didn't have sex again because that was going to be addictive and hard to get over once I left.

"Well, I came to buy an African American romance novel, but I guess I'll just watch the movie." Khari broke our trance, as he swung the door open and started talking loudly, as soon as he did.

I looked at him, and he was giving me his signature smirk.

"Shut up, Khari. You good by yourself for a few? We're just going down the street to handle a few things," Jahi informed me, and I nodded, before he kissed me again.

"Hey, Khari," I sang.

"Hey, Miss Thang. You are looking cute in them bell-bottoms. I knew your fine ass could pull it off," he complimented, as he walked up to me and hugged me, almost lifting my body from the countertop. "Can I kiss you, too?" he asked lowly, making me chuckle, before Jahi pushed him.

"Khari, why you always playing so much?" Jahi fumed, getting serious. I rolled my eyes. He had a quick temper.

"Baby bro, she was my bitch, before she was yours," Khari sassed.

"He does have a point." I nodded my agreement, as Jahi

looked between both of us and grilled us, causing us to fall out laughing.

"Yeah, aight. Bring yo' ass on," he fussed at Khari, before they left.

I quickly reached to my left for the store phone while pulling the small piece of paper from my pocket.

"Hello?" I heard her voice flow through the receiver, and I closed my eyes. "Lovie?" I immediately cringed at being called that shit again.

"I need your help."

"I told you that I had you whenever you decided to give me a call. By the way that you were acting, I didn't think it would be so soon, but what do you need?" she rushed out, as I heard rustling in her background like she was moving around.

"If you really want us to be-to be *sisters,* then I need your help getting an abortion."

"Wait, you're pregnant? From whom? Are you pregnant from Slim?"

"Do you want to help me or not?" I ignored her questions.

"I told you I'd do anything the night that I saw you. I took a big chance when I lied about who I was and snuck in that nigga's house for you. He's dangerous!" she exclaimed.

"I'm serious, Miranda," I warned.

"Just tell me how you want to do this, I'm in my car now." I heard her car come to life in the background.

"Meet me at the corner of that street where that old bookstore is that you took me to in twenty. I'll be at that park on the corner. Hurry up. I don't have much time." I hung up in her face, before she could respond. I hopped off the counter and threw down the magazine, before I went to the door. I looked both ways, as I slipped my oversized hoodie over my head. It was hot, as hell outside, but I had purposely worn it for this reason alone. I bolted out of the door and started down the street. I felt terrible for leaving Jahi and Khari the way that I was. They had been so nice to me, but I had to leave. I couldn't get attached to them or the life that was being provided to me. Even with Slim gone, I was still pregnant for him, and Jahi still had to marry someone else. So, I enjoyed my last week with him, before I made my move. I planned everything perfectly since I knew that he had stuff to handle today and couldn't stay with me at the bookstore. On my way to the park, I thought about how Miranda got to me. Was she the saving grace that I was crying for?

I was sitting in my bed after I heard Jahi bring some girl over, and I got up to shut my door since he was just standing there staring in my face. I didn't get a chance to see her because he had shoved her into his room, as soon as I heard the word "who."

"Ain't no dick on Earth that good," I grumbled because she was still loud as hell. I turned up the TV and finished my Sprite when the moaning finally stopped. I didn't know why, but I felt so jealous and pissed with Jahi. He was all in my face, trying to talk to me after our disastrous ass lunch, and after a week, he had given up and brought some girl over. This wasn't how stuff went in the books that I had read.

I thought I wanted him to leave me alone and that this was what was expected, but I was pissed. "Finally," I grumbled when I heard her stop moaning, and I chuckled when I thought about Jahi being a 'minute man' because their sex couldn't have lasted longer than fifteen to twenty minutes. I ran to the bathroom to vomit, and after brushing my teeth, I came back to the room, and I almost jumped out of my skin at the sight of Miranda standing there in a little pink dress and peering at me with those dark eyes that mirrored her brother's.

"Aww, Lovie, I missed you," she whispered, as she hugged me, and I froze. If she was here, was Slim here with her and the money? She must've felt me tense up because she pulled away from me and laughed a little. "Slim isn't with me. He's long gone. These African mother-fuckas busted down his door for money that he didn't have, and he left. But, before he left, he gave me one last call and told me that they took you. I tried my luck and went with the straight brother, and I found you. If you know where a back door is then we can leave." She looked around the room, as if the back door would be in there.

"Get out, before I scream," I warned her, causing her eyes to grow as large as saucers.

"You talk now?"

"Yes, now get out." I slapped her hands from my shoulders, before I sat back in the bed and pulled the comforter over my legs. She wasn't shit just like her brother.

"Did you not hear what I said, Lovie? Slim is gone. It can just be you and me. I don't have anyone else, and I need my sister. I just fucked somebody in hopes of getting to you, and it worked." Her eyes glazed over, as she spoke. But in my opinion, she didn't deserve anybody.

"One. Two."

"Okay! Okay! I'll leave!" She put her hands up in surrender. "Let me just leave you my number in case you ever need anything or want to talk. We can talk, can't we?" I glared at her, as she crept over to the desk like I had a loaded gun on her. She quickly wrote down her number on a sticky note, before putting it in a drawer of the desk. "I love you, Lovie. Please consider what I said. I can help you get away from these crazy ass niggas. Just think about what they'll do when they find out Slim ain't coming back with that money," she warned.

"Three," I said with finality, as she bolted out of the door. I had to laugh at how fast she had taken off, before I cut the TV off and let my mind roll over what would happen to me if Slim didn't come up with the money. I knew I for damn sure couldn't trust anybody. And was Slim really gone? I got my confirmation the next day in the car with Jahi.

Once I made it to the park, she was parked there in her white Altima, as she waited for me. When I got inside, she grinned at me and pulled me into a hug.

"I knew you would call me! It was just a matter of sooner or later!" she practically shouted.

"Let's just go." I sighed, as I sat back into the seat, as she pulled onto the road. "The clinic is on Colonial."

She talked a mile a minute about all of the stuff that we would do, as sisters. I missed Jahi and the calm silence that we had already. "Lovie, how did you start talking?"

I glanced at her smiling face and grew irritated already.

"I just did." I shrugged, trying to offer her something. She did just save my ass.

"Well, I'm glad that you did because that whole silence thing was annoying, as fuck. I can't believe that you're pregnant! Is it from Slim?" she asked, as I cut my eyes at her.

"No," I lied. She wasn't about to try and convince me to keep this baby.

"Slim is going to be pissed with your ass, girl." She finally rested against her seat and smiled.

I had to do a double take. "What?"

"Slim is going to be pissed that you've been giving the same niggas that ran him out of business his stuff," she spoke all casual, before pursing her lips and shaking her head.

"I—I thought you said that he was gone?" I stuttered, and she immediately let out a boisterous laugh.

"He is gone. I'm just taking you to him. He left me behind with a big, and I mean *big* stack of cash to get to you. It was just my luck that I picked the right brother to try and got some good ass dick out of the deal."

"Miranda, you can't do this. You can't take me to him," I panicked.

"Oh, but I can. And I will. You just better hope he don't give you an abortion himself or beat it out of you. You spread your legs for someone else. You're not special anymore, Lovie," she sighed and turned to me with a smile. I leaned over and put my head between my knees, as I started to hyperventilate.

Fuck that.

"Lovie, no!" she screamed, as I unlocked the door. I'd rather die than go back to Slim.

"Ahh!" we both screamed, as her tires got shot out. She was still trying to drive, before the back window got shot out, as well. I turned around and saw a black Jeep Trailhawk trailing us.

It wasn't long, before she couldn't drive anymore because of the tires and had to pull the car to the side of the road. I ducked when I heard a single shot ring out. My heart raced, as I heard footsteps approaching the car, and I looked to my left and saw Miranda's head against the steering wheel with a bullet between her open, dead, dark eyes.

"Ahhhhhhhh!" I screamed when the door was snatched open, and I was being yanked out by my arm.

I continued to scream as loud as I could with my eyes shut until I heard, "Shut the fuck up and get'cho sneaky ass in the truck, before it gets hot out here!" I opened my eyes, and Jahi was staring at me like he wanted to kill my ass.

"Wait!" I yelled, as he dragged me to the Trailhawk. I didn't know if he was going to kill me next or what.

He shoved me into the backseat, before getting in behind me. I looked to the front seat to see Khari with some kind of rifle in his hands while wearing a disappointed expression. Craig kept his eyes forward, as he pulled off onto the street like this shit was normal.

"You trying to leave me!" Jahi yelled, as I backed into the door.

"Jahi," Khari cooed and glanced back at him.

"Nah, fuck that! Answer my fucking question, Tove!" I hated when he yelled at me like that. With every word he spoke, his perfect canines that usually made him look so sexy, made him look more vicious.

"No!" I cried. He had just caught my ass red-handed trying to leave him, but I just felt like yes was the wrong answer. I was so scared and crying so hard that I was trembling.

"Then what the *fuck* was you just doing with yo' sneaky ass! You want to go back to Slim? 'Cause I'll find that nigga and bring him to you so that I can kill him in front of you. Is that what you want?"

"No." I shook my head, as tears streamed down my face. I didn't want to be anywhere near Slim.

"Oh, so you want me to keep him alive for you then?"

Even Khari had to turn around and cock his head at his nutty ass brother.

"I don't want him at all! I didn't *want* to leave!"

"Then why the *fuck* did I just catch you trying to go?"

"I—I," I started to hyperventilate again, leaning over to put my head between my knees.

"Alright Mkuu, that's enough," Khari intervened. "You gon' kill her."

"You almost killed me!" I lifted my head and shouted at his ass too.

"Bitch, don't disrespect me like that. One thing I'm not gon' do is miss my target." He pursed his lips, before rolling his eyes at me.

"Hello! I'm still waiting for an answer! And if you try that mute shit, I swear I'mma shake your little ass," Jahi fumed.

"I'm pregnant," I sobbed. "I just needed her help getting rid of it. I didn't know that she was going to try to take me to Slim. Y'all told me that he was gone."

"You don't think I fucking knew that shit, Tove? You think I took you to my family's doctor and they wouldn't tell me that? She told me, as soon as she walked out of the room. I just been waiting on you since she told me that you wanted to tell me. All you had to do was say the word and we could've handled that shit!" he fumed.

"Then why didn't you say anything?"

"Then why didn't *you* say anything, Tove? Or why did you think that I was dumb and didn't have surveillance in my house and check it regularly? *Especially* when a mad ass bitch that I didn't know walked through my house. I knew exactly what time she left out of my bedroom and exactly the time that she walked out of the front door," he revealed. "I had to find out from Khari that that was that nigga's sister, and I've been waiting on you this whole time to see if you was going to put me on game or try to dip on a nigga. And you dipped," he spoke disappointedly, before shaking his head and looking forward.

I didn't have anything to say.

Jahi texted something on his phone, and once we made it back to his house, Dr. Laissez was waiting to administer me the medicine herself. Jahi and I didn't speak or anything. He silently watched over me and slept in the bed with me for about a week, before sleeping in his own bed again. I didn't bother him, and he didn't bother me. I felt defeated and stupid because I could've gone to him the whole time. I had actually trusted Miranda of all people over Jahi and Khari.

But considering the circumstances, how was I supposed to know that I could trust him? All I'd had for years was myself. I was just trying to navigate shit the best way that I knew how.

Chapter Ten

JAHI

A month had passed, and Tove and I just kind of existed around one another. Neither of us really talked to one another. I worked most of the time, and she got stuff together for the bookstore's reopening since the progress had slowed down due to her wanting some other genres and first editions. With the books that she wanted first editions of, it would take a couple months to gather them all. With my family's connections and the ability to get them at a lower price but sell them for much more, it was a good investment. I had Djimon scouring to find them all.

Her little ass was picky and a little demanding mixed with OCD, but it was good to see her excited about something while she felt no one was paying attention to her. She rarely allowed herself to be happy or excited about anything.

We didn't talk unless it was necessary. I made sure to get

her a cellphone in case she ever needed me or wanted anything, but she never called or texted me. She ain't do shit but talk to Khari on it.

I never met anyone that was as stubborn as me, until her. I wanted to stay mad at her ass, but I couldn't. She never tried to leave again after her abortion, so I knew that she was just acting out of fear. Sometimes when I found myself frustrated with her, I had to remind myself that she was only twenty-three and that she was still figuring shit out. I had niggas everywhere looking for Slim, and I found it odd how he had basically disappeared. Nobody had ever gotten away from us for that long. But the minute he fucked up, I would have something hot waiting for that ass.

I walked outside by the swimming pool, as Tove just floated on top of the water and stared at the sky. If you didn't know her and how she made her eyes do that dead-like gaze, then you would swear that she was dead. It didn't even look like she was breathing, and she blinked her low eyes sparingly.

Her gaze fell to me, as I eased into the water, before she looked back at the sky.

"Don't do that," I instructed when it looked like she was about to get up so that she could leave. She rolled her eyes at me, before laying back and floating again. I admired how good she looked in the light blue two-piece swimsuit. Everything was covered except her stomach, but her body was so stacked that it didn't even matter. I would think her ass was fine in a burka though. Her hair was all around her, in wet locks like Medusa, as her ochre-colored skin glowed.

I leaned against the side of the pool, as I watched her. It was hard to bring my gaze anywhere else when I was around her.

"What do you want, Jahi?" she drawled out every word, as she kept her eyes to the sky. Sometimes I wished that she read books aloud just so I could hear her siren's song or feel that summer's breeze for longer periods of time.

"You."

"Whatever," she quipped.

"You think that you would be here if I didn't want you? I keep forgetting that I've never shown you that side of me."

She cut her eyes at me. "The yelling?"

"Lightweight." I shrugged.

She rolled her eyes. I decided then that she had been spending too much time with Khari. "Was there ever really a ransom, Jahi?" I found myself smirking at her country, drawled-out pronunciation of my name.

"No," I answered, honestly. "I made the price too high for him to pay so that I could have you."

She scoffed. "Because I'm an object."

"Because you're my person, and I knew it from the first time that I saw you. Do you want to go, Tove?" I feared her answer.

She was quiet for a moment, as she just stared without blinking.

"Do I have a choice?"

I felt a little rebuffed, but I nodded anyway, as she looked my way and our eyes locked.

"I don't want to go." She sighed, eyes going back to the sky. I looked up with her that time, and there wasn't much there besides a few stars.

"What does Jahi Ife Nuru mean?"

"Dignity, love, and light. Why?" I brought my eyes back to her.

"Knowing what names mean is my thing." She half shrugged, trying to stay afloat.

"What does Tove mean?" I asked, as I grabbed her arm and gently pulled her closer because she was floating to the further end of the pool. She didn't fight me, as I pulled her toward me.

"It means beautiful thunder."

"Fitting. Though in Africa, it means that God is good." Her eyes fell to me again, as her eyebrows rose slightly, before she quickly recovered. She seemed a little shocked that I knew what her name meant. "Why don't you believe that there's a God?" We were already on the outs, so asking what I wanted to know wouldn't make a difference at this point.

"Because what God would let me lose my mother at four-teen, get sold for cocaine by my father at sixteen, be a slave and raped regularly until I was twenty-three, and then conceive his child, while almost being delivered back to him with a bow?" I wanted to tell her that the last thing about being delivered back to Slim was on her and not God, but I declined. I took into consideration what she said, and though I was disturbed, I decided not to let her bask in her pain and her past. It wasn't conducive to her future.

"The same God that brought you to me. We all have our trials to endure. Some more than others. I can't relate to your trials because they surpass mine immensely, but I respect that you survived them."

She chuckled. "There ain't no God."

"All of that heavy literature that you read about life and the wonders of the world, and you've never even considered there being a God?"

"I have. But then I concluded that if there was one God or creator, then why are there so many different religions? I think people just want to believe in something bigger than themselves, or that there is this great plan for everyone, when we're all really alone and playing with a deck of cards dealt by the decisions made by our ancestors." She offered another half-shrug. I watched her pouty lips, as she spoke. I missed feeling them against mine since kissing wasn't something I did often, and her lips were so soft. I felt a surge of energy coming from them when I kissed her.

"I think there are so many religions or versions of God because everyone's perception of God and their experiences are different. And while I do feel that there is a great plan for everyone, I'm also not foolish enough to completely rely on that or feel like I shouldn't help God with my part in fulfilling my purpose in my plan."

"So, what's your perception of God?"

"I believe that there is a creator and that we should thank him daily for his provisions. While my family is mostly Christian, I don't have a specific faith or religion because I admire and take something from them all. And I'd never claim to be a religious or traditional man, just a grateful one. The problem involved is too vast for our limited minds. The human mind, no matter how highly trained, cannot grasp the universe," I continued.

"'We are in the position of a little child, entering a huge library whose walls are covered to the ceiling with books in many different tongues. The child knows that someone must have written those books. It does not know who or how.' Albert Einstein." She finished the quote with a smirk, as I gave a single nod. "He was somewhat of an atheist though."

"Nah, he was a pantheist. Einstein's God was the universe. He put his faith in its physics and quantum mechanics."

She gave a subtle nod.

"And what do you think about the theory of God being a woman?" she asked, tone laced with amusement.

"I believe that if God was a woman, then she would be you."

She stared at me long and hard, before she blinked, and I noticed a single tear roll down her face, before disappearing into the pool.

"Why would you say something like that?" she whispered, as her eyes narrowed.

"Because I would imagine her to be strong, powerful beyond measure, intelligent, a force to be reckoned with, beautiful, a little tortured, and gracious."

"A tortured God. I couldn't imagine." She grinned.

"After the way that this world turned out, I could see it." I nodded, as I brought her back to me again, allowing my fingers to rub the welt on her wrist. She looked startled at my noticing, but she quickly recovered again.

She was the exact definition of beautiful thunder and a representation of how God was good; she just didn't see it.

I lifted her from the water and pulled her body into mine.

"Jahi, let me go. You belong to someone else, and this is just fun for you, before you settle down and have the life that you're meant to."

"Even if I wanted to, I can't let you go. And you don't want to be let go of. You're just scared that if you put your trust in someone again that you'll get hurt." She was asking me to let her go but was contradicting herself by locking her thighs around my waist, as I held onto her.

"I will get hurt. I always do."

"Not by me, and I believe that I deserve the benefit of the doubt."

"And your wife to be?" she asked, as I pulled her wet top from her body and she helped me do it.

"I'm with her now. In the end, I have the final say."

She looked off to the side, before I brought her face back to me by her chin. I kissed her and pulled her bottoms off of her, again with her help.

"You make me complex and emotional," she spoke against my lips.

"And you make me vulnerable and complete." I freed myself from the swim trunks, before poking at her entrance.

"Don't say what you don't mean."

"I mean that."

I groaned at the feel of entering her. I had fucked some females just to bust a nut since we had been on the outs, but nothing came close to her pussy, and I definitely wasn't having raw sex with them. I had only had her once, but that was enough to miss it. Sex with her felt spiritual. It felt like something to be devoted to and to be thankful for.

I watched, as her head went back, as she wrapped her arms around my neck while her hands dug into my hair. I rhythmically pumped in and out of her, as she finally met my gaze and moaned against my lips. She let me know, without words, that we had been speaking the same language all along. That we were on the same page with how we felt for one another.

"Jahi," she moaned my name, only making me go harder, forcing a set of waves to form and splash all around us. She bit my bottom lip and sucked on it, before tossing her head back again, and if I wasn't fucking her, I could still cum off visuals alone, as her head went back and her perfect breasts bounced in my face, while she bit her bottom lip and chanted my name until she was shivering.

I was glad that I gave Barika the day off because the next thing I knew, I was carrying Tove through the house, soaking wet, before we made it to the living room and to the sofa.

I grabbed a handful of her wet hair, as I stroked into her from the back, and she accepted every thrust and welcomed it with a moan.

"Harder!" she called out, as she started tossing her ass

back on me. I was trying to go gentle on her, but I started to pound into her, per request, and that automatically sent her into a fit of shivers. She came long and hard, before we took it to the shower.

"Wait a minute, fuck!" I groaned, as I tried to take my dick out of her mouth. She had my ass cornered in the shower, as she sucked the life out of me. I was going to kill her if she ever told anyone how she had me trying to grip the walls and get away from her. I was a grown ass man and she had me running from some head. She wouldn't let up until she had sucked me up and swallowed everything.

"Why are you looking at me like that?" she asked, as she crawled into my lap on the bench in the shower and started stroking me back to life just that fast.

"What the fuck you mean why I'm looking at you like this? Nigga, I'm in love!"

Her head fell back, as she started to laugh hard until she snorted, then slapped her hand over her mouth and whined. I laughed at her reaction because she really hated that shit, but it was cute as fuck when she did it. She rarely laughed or smiled, so I tried to etch this moment into my memory and simultaneously tried to figure out ways to make it happen more frequently. It was like my life flashed before me, when I imagined having her like this forever. I couldn't see a better future for myself.

"Fuck, *wewe ni wangu*," my face contorted, as she lowered herself onto me and I gripped her hips, as she bounced so that she wouldn't slip and so that I could have something to hold on to. She had my ass speaking Swahili to her and her brows tented in confusion. I took turns sucking on each hardened nipple, as a means to avoid moaning too loud, inadvertently making her moan louder.

After more shower sex, bed sex, kitchen sex, and shower sex again, she laid her head on my chest while eating Hot Cheetos, as we watched TV. Her wild, blow-dried hair was everywhere and blocking my view unless I held it down with my hand. Her head randomly popped up, as she turned to face me, looking like she was in deep thought.

"What?"

"Can you teach me how to shoot?" She bore into me with those low green eyes that were light and full of life at that moment. Nothing like the first time I saw her.

"Uhh—depends."

"On what?"

"Are you trying to shoot me?"

"No." She laughed.

"Then sure. I'll teach you in the morning. I'm off. We can use Djimon for target practice." She laughed and seemed satisfied, before she turned back around and put her big ass hair in my way again. Her head popped up again, as she turned to me, making me chortle. It was like trying to watch TV with a child that kept talking.

"What?"

"Did Khari really know what he was doing that day that he shot at that car, or was he taking a chance?" she asked, as she ate them nasty ass chips and licked her red-tipped fingers.

I looked her over briefly and noticed that she was gaining a little weight, but I didn't mind it.

"Khari can shoot blindfolded with his hands tied behind his back and still not miss. You were in good hands," I assured her. She seemed satisfied again, as she nodded then turned back around to watch TV.

It wasn't long after she finished those chips, brushed her teeth, and washed her hands, before I heard her breathing heavily. I peeped down, and she was asleep. I eased her to the center of the bed, before cutting everything off and pulling her into me; wild hair in my face and all.

"*Wewe ni wangu*," I told her again, before kissing her lips. I pulled her as close as I could, before falling asleep with her.

———

"Open your eyes!" I chuckled, as Tove raised the gun with two hands, and she squeezed her eyes shut.

"Um, Jahi, I'm not comfortable with this at all," Djimon said through shaky breaths, as he held the target to his right.

"It'll be fine, Djimon! We can have you patched right up if things go bad." I waved him off, making his eyes go big. He usually would read off an itinerary while holding the target for Khari and me, but Tove had his ass shook... and rightfully so.

"What!" he shouted.

"I can't do this with him talking," she fussed.

"Oh, honey, him talking is the least of your worries," Khari sat in a chair next to me in the backyard, as we watched the pending homicide. Barika was in the house praying loud as fuck, only making the situation more amusing. I laughed at the fact that Khari really thought that Tove was his personal doll. He had her dressed like she was going hunting or some shit with duck boots on, jeans that hugged every curve, a black muscle shirt, and a blue and black flannel on top. Her hair was still big, wavy, and untamed—I had decided then that I liked it best that way.

"Oh, suck a dick, Khari," she tossed over her shoulder, making him gasp dramatically.

"I liked you better when you were mute, bitch!"

"You take it in the ass while spreading your own ass cheeks. You're the bitch!"

"Cunt!"

"Stank twat!"

"I'm not even the bottom when I fuck, thank you! I'm the one delivering the strokes," he spoke proudly while thrusting his hips and using his arms for emphasis, making me frown.

"Enough of this shit!" I intervened, as they both cackled. They had this brother and sister-like banter going on every time they were around one another, since the day he shot at that car. They acted as if they couldn't stand one another but couldn't be separated either. They had to talk to and see each other almost every day.

"Shoot the target, Tove. With your eyes open!" I yelled.

"Sorry, Djimon, I really do like you and when you help me with the store." She apologized, before she squeezed the trigger with her eyes snapping shut, but Khari was on his feet already, jerking her arms in the right direction since she was aiming straight for Djimon's chest. I sat back amused, as Djimon looked like he pissed himself, and his knees buckled together.

"Damn, bitch, you can't fight or shoot. What can you do besides read, look pretty, and wear the fuck out them jeans?" Khari griped, and she heard me stifle a laugh, before she shot me a glare over her shoulder.

"I can suck a *mean* dick," she gave me a devious grin, forcing me out of my chair and to my feet.

"Alright! Funny shit is over. Let me show you how to do this, baby." I came behind her and placed my hands above hers over the gun. I knew if her ass told Khari exactly what happened in that shower, then I would never live it down.

"Mhm," she hummed, as Khari looked confused, before he caught on and laughed.

"Are your eyes open?" I looked down at her and they were. As she nodded, big ass hair brushing my chin. I was done fucking with Djimon for the day and had pinned the target to the board. I actually needed my annoying assistant.

"Mhm."

I let her hands go, as mine hovered above hers, and when she pulled the trigger, she hit the bullseye.

"I did it!" She turned around wildly and jumped up and down with the gun in her hand, making me, Khari, and Djimon duck. We heard Barika start to pray louder.

"Hardly! Put that shit down! Talking about I almost killed

you! We're even if that's the case!" Khari fussed, and they went back to arguing.

I shook my head, before reclaiming my chair and taking a sip of my water. I watched, as Khari took over. I could shoot, and I never missed, but I'd be lying if I said that Khari wasn't the better shooter.

"You're falling in love, Jahi," Djimon spoke, as he took the seat next to me. I didn't even realize that I was smiling at her until then. I would've never thought that she would've opened up that way.

"I am."

"You can't. You have a responsibility to your family. They've given you everything, and they always sing your praises. You should at least show your gratitude by respecting their wishes and traditions," he warned. "I like her, Jahi, I really do. But she doesn't fit into your life or your plans." I could've been offended, but I wasn't. That wouldn't be Djimon if he wasn't warning someone or trying to stick to strict guidelines.

"Then I'll make her fit," I challenged. I couldn't let her go and wasn't shit going to take her away from me. Not even my last name.

Chapter Eleven

TOVE

THREE MONTHS LATER...

This was *not* Jahi. Not even the 8.9 version. Maybe this was Mkuu. And maybe this is what happened when a Nuru man felt disrespected or protective. I watched in terror, as Jahi pummeled Deon's face repeatedly. No one would touch him or pull him away. I didn't know if it was the fear or the power that Jahi had that made it that way.

"Come on, Mkuu." Khari finally started to pull Jahi away from Deon. Once Khari stepped in, the guards slowly made their way in an attempt to help pull him away. Deon looked almost unconscious with his eyes immediately starting to swell. He had gashes on his face like Jahi hit him with something other than his fists, but he hadn't. I was glad that we were in the storage room where we kept the first editions sealed away until it was time for them to be purchased.

Khari spoke roughly to Jahi in a hushed tone, as Jahi's chest heaved up and down, and he grunted his responses. I could tell that he was trying to bring him to his senses. He was holding the back of his head like a coach about to put their star player in the game. They were right in front of me, but Khari's words were indecipherable. Jahi's broad chest heaved up and down, and he looked like a demon with Deon's blood on his clothes. I felt my eyes grow larger when he turned his head my way.

"Tove," he spoke in a gruff tone, as he held an extended hand out to me. I don't even think he realized that his hands still had blood on them. My first instinct was to recoil, making him frown.

"You scared of me, Tove?" he asked in a softer tone, and he seemed hurt by my actions, hand still extended. I watched Khari give me a subtle nod. *Did he think that I was fucking crazy?* He wanted me to leave with this giant after watching him hulk out.

"No," I answered meekly, as I hesitantly took his hand. After all, he was defending me. I hadn't had someone to defend me or look out for me since my ma passed away. I felt bad like somehow it was my fault that he was fighting his associate. He stared at me a moment longer, and I relaxed as much as I visibly could, before he pulled me with him, away from Khari and the guards and through the back entrance where he had parked. His eyes were pensively on me, as he opened the door for me, allowing me to slip in, as I held up my floor-length, black, silk dress, with the thigh split and exposed back. He had looked so handsome earlier in his tux. He still did, even with the visible blood splatters across the white shirt.

"You okay?"

"Yeah, I'm fine."

"I love you, Tove Monroe," he told me all of a sudden, as his eyes stayed on the road. I wasn't ready to hear those words. Not now, at least not under these circumstances.

"I love you too, Jahi Nuru," I responded. I wasn't lying. I had fallen in love with Jahi long ago.

He seemed satisfied with my response, as he grabbed my hand with his blood-stained one, as he drove us home, and I mulled over the night.

It was the night before the grand reopening of Cover Cove, the bookstore that was now mine and renamed, and a small crowd of influential people wanted to hold an auction for some of the first editions that we had acquired for the store. I was nervous and excited, but I was ready. I was doing something that involved my passion for books.

"You look so fucking sexy," Jahi whispered in my ear, causing me to shiver a little, before looking up at him and taking in his dapper appearance. Tailored black tux and white button-down, with his Christian Louboutin dress shoes and a nice watch. I thought that the event would be more casual until Khari burst into the house with an evening gown.

"Not bad yourself." I smirked, before we kissed.

"Unt un, miss ma'am! I may be the host, but this is your store, and everyone is thrilled to meet the new owner!" Khari fussed, causing me to grow nervous and my stomach to form knots.

"Go ahead. Enjoy yourself and mingle." Jahi gave a backwards nod, before kissing me again.

"Congratulations, Tove!" Deon said, as he walked up with some girl, before Khari could take me away. Every time that we saw him, he was with another woman. He gave me an outstretched hand, and I hesitantly and quickly shook it. Deon always made me uncomfortable, ever since the first day that I met him. And it wasn't just the gun that he had trained on me. He looked at me how Slim looked at me the first night that we met.

"Thank you!" I accepted graciously with a fake smile plastered across my face, figuring that maybe his ass would buy a book. None of these first editions were cheap. I even had an 1866 First Edition of Lewis Carroll's Alice Adventures in Wonderland in a slipcase for fourteen thousand dollars.

"Let's go," Khari spoke, as he looked Deon up and down, before whisking me away to mingle. Khari hardly ever acknowledged him. I had felt eyes on me all night, and if they weren't the proud looks from Jahi that made my cheeks warm, then they were the skeevy inducing ones from Deon. The man made my skin crawl.

"Hey, Tove! Damn, you are wearing that dress!" I didn't even have to turn around to know that it was Ashley. When I did turn around, I watched, as she sauntered toward me with her thick arms wide open while wearing a deep red gown. She looked so pretty, and the dress looked like it was poured over her curves.

"Hey. You look gorgeous," I complimented and hugged her.

"Mhm." Khari hummed, before pulling her away from me and into a lip lock.

"Slut," I called out and chuckled once he gave me the bird. And he had the nerve to talk about me kissing on Jahi.

"Soooo, Tove." Ashley gave me a smirk.

"Yesss," I sang.

"I heard that you have the first edition of Under the Sunset by Bram Stoker that is signed by the author, who did not make it a habit to sign his work, so that makes this one extra special."

"You may have heard right," I raised an eyebrow.

"I'll pay extra to have it taken out of the auction. My father loves his work, and I need this." She looked at me pleadingly with her hands clasped together.

"Eight grand, Sugartits," I bargained. If I was going to take it out of auction, it was going to be worth my while.

Her lips pursed, as she leaned over into Khari's side and said, "She's sexy as hell when she's negotiating."

"Mhm." He hummed with a smirk, causing me to do that ugly laugh where my head falls back.

"You got a deal, pretty bitch."

"I'll be right back!" I threw over my shoulder, before excitedly pulling the keys to the storage room from my clutch. I was so giddy and excited that I didn't even notice him following me into the storage room.

"Ahh!" I screamed when I felt his presence.

"Deon, you scared the shit out of me. Can I help you?" I turned back around to open the airtight glass case. I pulled the book from it and began to package it in the smaller glass casing. The glass was for *display purposes, and the books were kept in a cool, dark storage room to keep out the humidity and sunlight. And keeping the books in airtight containers prevented the time riddled pages from molding.*

"You can give me some of that five-million-dollar pussy."

"What?" I froze, as I looked over my shoulder to see if he was serious. His eyes were on my ass, as he chewed on a toothpick.

"You heard what the fuck I said. Got niggas buying you stores and shit and not getting their ransom money. So, I definitely need that kind of pussy in my life." He grabbed his crotch, as he stepped toward me.

"Get the fuck back, before I scream, creep ass nigga." I threatened, as he was walking me into the glass container that contained all of the books.

"Just give me a lil' taste. Damn. Don't be stingy like you wasn't just a hoe. Jahi got you thinking you better than what you are, but you got the game fucked up because Jahi getting married, baby girl, and it ain't to yo' ass. You should be happy that a rich nigga wanna even sniff that worn-out cat. Gone 'head and top a nigga off or something."

"Get out right now!" I snapped, as I pointed at the door. I gasped, as he brought his hand around my throat and started to choke me, while trying to force me to my knees.

"Or what, bitch?" He started to try and free himself, as he undid his zipper. I tried to scream, but he squeezed tighter. My nails clawed at his hand that was around my throat, as I fought to stay on my feet. I felt myself mentally trying to shut down and bring back up my fortress, but I fought that feeling. I would not allow Deon to make me a victim again.

WHAM!

Out of nowhere, Jahi appeared and started to deliver blow after blow, but Deon was dazed after the first blow. I backed all the way into the cabinet and shrunk to the ground.

"You okay?" Khari asked me, lifting me right back up, and it was then that I realized that he must've walked in with Jahi.

"Y-yeah," I stuttered. I wanted to ask if anyone was going to stop him, but I got my answer, as the guards and Khari stood around with their hands in their pockets until Khari felt it was enough and decided to pull Jahi back. I guess the point of it being enough was when Deon was on the brink of death.

Now I was in the car with... shit, Jahi, Ife, Mkuu, somebody, and I was scared. This wasn't a regular beat down. Deon had clearly lost the battle and the war, but Jahi just kept pounding at his ass repeatedly. I flinched a little, as the first power-packed blow replayed in my mind.

I was quiet, as Jahi opened the door for me. He and Khari had made sure that I never touched a door when with them. I was glad that Barika was more than likely resting already because seeing him covered in blood like this would send her into a fit of prayers. We walked up the stairs and into the bedroom that we now shared.

He wore this expression like he was still trying to come down from the adrenalin that coursed through his veins when he hulked out. His chest was still puffed out and he wore a pensive, dark glare. But he was still handsome, even with the scowl. His beard was neat, and his hair was still in a smoothed back, low ponytail that hung down his back. He was a beautiful nightmare.

I decided to take control, as I grabbed his hand and pulled him into the bathroom.

He stared at me, as I took my time undressing him and putting all of his stuff away, so that it could be sent off to be cleaned. I took his watch from his wrist, cleaned it free of blood, and placed it in his casing. He even stared at me, as I got undressed and put my dress, jewelry, and shoes away.

I cut on the shower, before grabbing his hand and pulling him in with me. I began to wash his hands, and as soon as I was finished, I gasped when he quickly picked me up into his arms, and he had his mouth on mine, before he slid deep inside me. No foreplay or warning, but my tortured ass was wet from the moment he started staring at me.

"I love you," he groaned against my lips, as he gave me long, slow, strong strokes, bringing me to my first orgasm, before I could even reply.

"I love you too," I whined, as I trembled on him.

"*Wewe ni wangu*! You hear me?" he asked.

I nodded and moaned out, "Yes!" After him saying it to me so much, I finally asked what it meant, and he was telling me that I was his. And I was. I delighted in the love bites and hickies that he littered across my skin and the way he was molding my pussy to be the perfect fit for him and him alone. I even delighted in the gentle nibbles that he would give my nipples while delivering deep strokes.

"Jahi," I whined, as he transferred his energy to me, and we spoke in our dialect. He was telling me that he needed more, so I pulled his head back and kissed him with everything that I had to give. I tightened my pussy's grip on his dick, as he moaned loudly into my mouth. This was my 8.9 Jahi, and I felt the monster that had taken over, leaving.

"You're mine too," I spoke against his lips, as he brought my body into a hug while he fucked me until I was spent and felt like I'd slip into unconsciousness if he ripped another orgasm from me.

I was relieved when he slowed down after he came because he had kept pumping through the first two nuts that he had.

He held my body up because I was so spent, as he began to bathe me and then himself.

"Thank you for protecting me," I told him once we were out of the shower and I was snuggled under his muscular arm, as he sat back and flicked through the channels on the television, not really paying attention to any of it.

"Don't ever thank me for that. You protect the ones that you love and care about." I nodded, as I just sat there and stared at him. I wished that he had been around my whole life, and then maybe at times I wouldn't feel so damaged. He had a clear set of morals that he lived by, and I loved that about him.

He looked down at me, before giving me a kiss and then returning his gaze to the TV. "I'm sorry for fucking up your night. I know it meant a lot to you, and you looked sexy as fuck doing your thing."

I blushed. "Thank you, and you didn't fuck up my night. Deon did."

"Yeah, but I pulled you out of there."

"The night wasn't going to be the same for me after that anyway, baby. Especially not without you." I ran my fingers through his hair, when he laid his head on my lap.

"Can I have some more pussy?" His voice vibrated off my thighs, making me titter.

"Baby, you broke my pussy in the shower. I might go into a coma if you fuck me again."

"Let me eat it then." He kneeled in front of me and started to pull my panties down without waiting for a response.

"Now, that's no problem."

―――――

My head popped up at the sound of my alarm going off. After finding my phone on the nightstand and silencing it, I felt around for Jahi, but he wasn't in bed. I smelled the scent of Barika's cooking and figured he must've been downstairs helping her with dishes or something. He had been helping her around the house whenever he could, ever since he saw us making the bed together.

I groaned at the pain between my thighs because of Jahi. I bit my lip, as flashbacks played through my mind.

He tried to keep eating me until I damn near blacked out. I had to snatch his head away by his hair to get him to stop. Then he had the nerve to tell me, "Ain't nobody supposed to stop just because you cummin' and shaking and shit. Bring yo' lil vibrating ass back here."

After taking another shower, brushing my teeth, and flossing, I settled on denim shorts, a fitted t-shirt, and some comfortable tennis shoes, since I was going to be on my feet all day, and I was ready to go. I left my hair wild and just tossed it forward and then back, before I stepped into the hallway. I was making my way to the stairs when I heard voices. I quickly went the rest of the way and followed the voices to the large dining room that had a table that could sit eighteen people. Jahi said it was for when his family held events at his house.

"Jah—" my words were cut off when I saw his parents. Barika, Jahi, and a beautiful girl that wore a blue, yellow, gray and black khanga. Her beautiful auburn skin glowed, and she looked like she could be a model.

My heart dropped when I saw her hand in Jahi's. He quickly snatched his away. Barika looked at me with sorrow-filled eyes while she stirred the pot to whatever she was about to serve.

"Oh, come and meet Jahi's fiancée, Toby." His mother waved me over, and I saw Jahi shoot daggers her way with his eyes.

"Hello, who are you?" the girl asked in her thick accent—almond-shaped eyes on me, as she smiled at me. I didn't miss her looking at me from head to toe though.

I felt tears spring to my eyes, before I took off down the corridor.

"Tove!" he called after me, but I kept running until I was outside with Craig.

"Please get me out of here!" I pleaded, as he looked at me with sympathetic eyes. "Please, Craig!" I screamed when he hesitated. He quickly helped me in the back of the Escalade, before hopping in and taking off. I looked through the back window and saw Jahi standing there and his fiancée running up right behind him. I turned my head and bit back tears because I refused to let another man break me. I knew that this was a possibility, so catching feelings for him was on me, even though he lied and said that we would be good. My heart felt like it was burning in my chest and pounding like it wanted to break free and run back to him. He had just told me that he loved me the night before, and now this.

I took deep breaths and composed myself, before I could tell Craig that I wanted to be dropped off at the bookstore. I couldn't afford to let heartbreak take this moment away from me. I had already lost so much in the past. So, I closed my eyes until I no longer felt like crying, and I dead myself inside a little. It was the only way that I knew how to get by and cope.

"Hi!" I spoke to my team, as I walked into the building. Some old faces with some new amongst them. Nobody ever brought up seeing me in here with Slim before, and I was glad for that.

"Hey."

"Hi."

"Hello," they spoke in unison.

"I know that this is a reopening, and it's the first day, so we all may be a little nervous and busy, but everything is going to be *fine,* and if you need anything or if you're feeling overwhelmed, then let me know. I'm always available to talk or assist you. This store won't run well if you aren't well. You guys have a great day, and I appreciate you!" Some of them cooed, thanked me, and told me to have a great day, as well.

I sat at a small round table in the cafe section and just tried processing my thoughts and clearing my mind.

Did he know they were coming? Why would he carry on with me if he was still getting married? Why would he tell me that he loved me?

"It's on the house for the boss lady, of course." A guy named Daniel set a cup of coffee in front of me. I looked up into his handsome face and smiled. He was an around the way, the guy next door, type of handsome with his medium brown skin, dark eyes, and white smile with a gap between his front teeth. He wasn't the type of handsome or beautiful that Jahi was, but still handsome, nonetheless.

"Oh, I'm sorry, I don't drink coffee." I frowned, making him chuckle.

"I know. That's why I made you a hot chocolate with whip cream and a sprinkle of cinnamon."

"Wait—how did you—?"

"Well, when we were setting things up, and you were taste testing the pastries and foods, you would order a hot chocolate with whip cream and a sprinkle of cinnamon, and I never forget a face nor a drink order."

"Aw, thank you!" I placed a hand over my heart. It felt good knowing that someone was paying attention to the small things. The regulars were going to love him since he could remember an order like that, even down to the cinnamon.

"No problem. So, where's your boyfriend? The big guy that you're always with? He's not here for your opening day?" He took a seat next to me, and I sighed.

"He's not my boyfriend."

"Oh, I could've sworn that—you know what? Not my business." He chuckled with his hands up in surrender, making me laugh at him. "It's opening time, boss lady." He nodded toward the door, and a line was forming already.

I took a deep breath, before going to open the door while hoping that keeping busy would keep my mind off of Jahi. I didn't have anywhere to go, but I did have some money that I made from the auction, so I could probably use that to move out. I didn't really know what I was going to do, but I did know that I wasn't going to live there with Jahi and his fiancée.

It was busy as fuck, and I wanted to kick my shoes off as soon as the last customer walked out of the door. I never knew that a bookstore could get so much traffic. I think part of that was people wanting to see what the Nuru men had invested in and crafted.

Jahi and Khari had handmade every white oak bookshelf in here, and they moved at an incredibly fast pace. They even were hands-on and helped me paint the walls a pastel blue. I felt like the soft blue was a relaxing color while reading or shopping.

Jahi. I huffed.

"I'm sorry, we're closed. We'll be back open tomorrow at nine a.m.," I threw over my shoulder while putting some books away, mentally cursing myself for not locking the door as soon as the last person left.

"Good thing we aren't here for the books," I heard Khari's voice, instantly making a smile spread across my face. I turned around to see Khari, Ashley, Aniya and Antony.

"Hey y'all!" I was excited to see them. I had hung out with them plenty, but it was always a good time that made you want more. They were so fun and free, and we were always finding something different to get into.

"Hey y'all!" They mocked me in unison, and I gave them the bird.

"What are y'all doing here, and what is all of this?" I asked, as I looked at the ring light and black kit.

"Wellll," Aniya sang. "I work for *Melanated Magazine,* and I told them that I had a new black business owner to interview.

"And I," Antony joined with a finger lifted. "Just so happened to be obsessed with trying to do her makeup."

"Oh no," I whined with my hands flying up to cover my face. I don't know if it was because of my past or just being shy, but I didn't like attention.

"Oh hush, girl. It'll be fun!" Khari waved me off. Our eyes locked for a moment, and the way he looked at me let me know that he knew about everything that went on this morning. Maybe this is why he brought everyone here to try to cheer me up. Khari and I had an unspoken language too, but it was more so a sibling type of thing. We could share a glance and communicate everything that we were thinking or feeling.

"Alright," I obliged. I wasn't in a rush to get back to Jahi's home anyways. I was going to have to get as much as I could and then go get me a room at a hotel.

"Ouch!" I shrieked, as Antony's rough ass tweezed my eyebrows.

"Be quiet. It's only one little stray hair. I would kill for these brows, honey," he sassed, as I stared into his face and his slanted eyes with lush lashes were narrowed in on my eyebrows.

"Okay, can we proceed?" Aniya asked.

"Yes." I gave a curt nod.

I looked to my left and saw Khari and Ashley's asses eating the few pastries that didn't get sold.

"Fat ass!" I called out to Khari.

"You're the one who went up a pants size, Hot Cheeto eating hoe," he snapped.

"Hh!" I gasped. "Khari you said that you'd never bring that up!"

"I lied. Don't play with me, play with ya cat. Fine ass," he mumbled the last part, making me titter, as Antony huffed and frowned at me because I kept talking and moving.

"Sorry," I whined, before his eyes roamed my face and he gave me a little grin.

"Ookkayyy," Aniya interceded. "What do you love about books?"

"That's a pretty general question. This should be easy. They take your mind away from reality. There were many days where I felt like I was dying inside of my reality, but I had a book to take me to Paris, to a love scene, to a beach, to see the Aurora Borealis or some kind of paradise. Books have been a sanctuary for me. A protector of my mind while my body endured the pain."

Everyone was quiet and just stared at me, as Aniya enthusiastically wrote.

"What's the name of your favorite book and if you could give me a quote from that, what would it be?" she asked when she finally looked back up from her notepad.

"I would have to say *She's Come Undone* by Wally Lamb has to be my favorite book. A quote from that book," I pondered. "A quote that I love from that book is, 'Love is like breathing. You take it in and let it out'." I exhaled, trying to release my love for Jahi. My eyes found Khari's and he looked sad for me.

"That's a good one. But not my favorite from that book." I heard *his* voice, before I saw him. I didn't even hear him come in. "A better one, to me, is 'Accept what people offer. Drink their milkshakes. Take their love'." He came into view, and my heart started to do that pounding shit that I had been trying to avoid all day. He looked so sexy yet simple, as he dressed down in the gray joggers with the gray matching hoodie and some Retro Jordans. His tall body stepped closer into the light.

"'He's splitting me open, I thought. He'll break me, and then I'll die'," I countered, as he nodded and then stepped closer. Antony had moved to the side, and everyone had stopped moving just to watch us.

"That's a good one too. You almost got me, but I'd counter that with 'if you risked love, it took you wherever you wanted to go. If you repressed it, you ended up unhappy'."

"'I thought about how love was always the thing that did that—smashed into you, left you raw. The deeper you loved, the deeper it hurt'." I tilted my head, eyes briefly rolling upward to divert the tears that had sprung to them. He was now hovering over me and the stool that I sat in.

"'I know it's a crock of shit. I ain't offering you happily-ever-after. I'm offering you... happily-maybe-sometimes-ever-after. Sort of. You know, with warts and shit'."

"You already have a happily-ever-after, Jahi. And it ain't with me," I croaked, breaking our recitation of quotes. Him reading and being able to recite my favorite book had me on the verge of breaking out into sobs. Loving him while he belonged to someone else was torture.

"But that's not what I told you, huh, Tove?" he asked, as he pulled a box from his pocket and kneeled on one knee in front of me.

"Jahi, what are you doing?" I whined. "I don't deserve to be played with anymore. Just go do what you have to do and let me go." The tears that I had been holding back began to roll down my cheeks. I would apologize to Antony later.

Jahi shook his head dismissively, before speaking. "I told

you that I wouldn't hurt you, and I meant that. I told you that I deserved the benefit of the doubt, and you gave me that and stayed with me. This morning when my parents brought that woman to my house and demanded that I marry her, I was grabbing her hand to let her down gently and to apologize for her time being wasted. She had travelled across the world just for me to tell her that I had already found my wife and that hopefully one day she would find her husband, but it wasn't going to be today—at least not with me."

Tears streamed down my face, and I was silent. I had no words, and it wasn't from torture. It was because my heart was so filled with love, and I didn't know how to translate that. I had never been loved by a man like this, so I didn't know the language.

"Will you marry me, Tove Monroe?" he asked, as he removed the ring from the box, grabbed my hand and hovered the ring over the tip of my ring finger.

"Yes," I croaked. I saw him exhale for the first time since he had kneeled in front of me. He slid the princess cut, canary diamond ring, set in platinum, down my finger, before standing up and hugging me, taking my body off of the stool with him. Everyone cooed, and I looked over Jahi's shoulder at Khari and caught him wiping his tears, as he held his phone up recording us. In fact, there wasn't a dry eye in the room.

"You mean to tell me that this lil' fine motherfucka about to be my sister now?" Khari sassed.

"Fuck yeah," Jahi retorted, causing us all to laugh.

. . .

It took a while, but Antony finished my makeup and Aniya finished her interview and took pictures of me, before we left.

"You hungry?" Jahi quizzed, as he drove.

"Yep. Starved."

"What do you want to eat? You want to get dressed and go out to celebrate?"

I immediately started to shake my head no. Even with my new-found freedom, it didn't take long for me to realize that I was mostly a homebody. If I had books and Jahi, I was satisfied.

"Um... I never had Tanzanian food before. I think I want to try some of that. It always smells really good when Barika makes y'all some. But I don't want to bother her. It's late."

"Okay, I'll make you some."

"The hell you will!" My head snapped into his direction. Every meal he ate was prepared for him. Jahi was very spoiled, and I never saw him put a pot on the stove. He wasn't about to fuck me up.

"Nigga, I can cook. The fuck? I got three meals down pat." He boasted, causing me to laugh until I snorted, which made him laugh harder. He literally said three whole meals. "Just take yo' ass upstairs, take your shower, and I'll make you something."

I eyed him suspiciously. "Alright. But only because I'm still high from you proposing."

"Damn, it's like that?"

"Mhm. So, how did your parents take you turning her

down?" I really kind of felt bad for her being that she traveled far as hell just to get sent right back.

"They don't like it. They're pissed. But it's not about them." He shrugged. "It's about my happiness, and that involves you, not some woman that I don't know. They lucky that I was feeling generous today. I think you're changing my ass." He kissed the back of my hand like he always did.

"Hey, Jahi?"

"Hmm?"

"I love you, Jahi Ife Nuru, sometimes Mkuu."

"And I love you, Tove Monroe Nuru."

My heart warmed at the thought of having his last name.

"You ready?" he asked, as I nodded while staring into the bowl. We were in the sitting room watching TV, before we sat at the floor table. Sometimes if we wanted to catch a movie, which was rare, we would do it and eat in here.

"What is it?" I frowned, and he mushed me.

"Alright, so this is called mchicha. It's really popular in Tanzania."

"Where's the meat? I like meat."

"I know you do, dome doctor. But this is a vegetarian meal."

I slapped his arm, as he laughed.

"Okay, and what's that?" I pointed at the white stuff.

"This is ugali, you eat these two together. You take a bit of the ugali and roll it until it forms a ball, then you make an indentation with your thumb like this." He demonstrated, as he molded the substance between his fingers. "And now it's like an edible spoon. See how it's not sticking to my fingers?"

"Mhm."

"That means yo' nigga makes the best ugali around," he boasted with a cocky lopsided grin.

"Shut up." I chuckled, as I watched him dig the ugali into the m-word stuff, before bringing it to my lips.

"Mmm, wait, this is really good." I moaned and nodded, as my eyes rolled back. When my eyes went back to normal, he was proudly nodding his head. It took me a second to get it down, but eventually, I was rolling, denting, dipping and eating all by myself.

"This is why I'm getting fat. Always eating good shit over here," I complained, as I stuffed something he called mandazi into my mouth. The shit was comparable to a good ass beignet.

"That's happy weight, baby." He responded, eyes on the TV, as he stuffed his face. I just took a second to look him up and down and marvel at him. He had really come in and flipped my whole world upside down. I was no longer the strong and silent Lovie that I had to be. Dealing with Jahi sent me through an array of emotions that I hadn't allowed myself to feel for seven years. I was happy, content, vulnerable, sometimes I even cried, and I was in love *Tove*, all the time.

Chapter Twelve

JAHI

A WEEK LATER...

"The fuck is this supposed to be about?"

"The hell if I know. I was trying to be laid up all day, and then Baba called me saying that it was important," Khari spoke, as he put lip balm on while looking in his visor.

We had just pulled up to my father's main office, and you only got called here when you fucked up. So, I already knew that this nigga was about to be in a pissy mood. Besides me declining to marry the woman they brought here, I didn't know what else it could've been because everything was going smooth. I handled all of my shit on the East side of town, and everybody was paying up on time. We even replaced Slim with another, more solid nigga since Slim left all of his hoes and most of his drugs behind.

"Nigga, is you done?" I spat, as I saw Khari pulling out some silver thing to use on his eyelashes.

"You know a bitch has to be presentable everywhere he goes," he sassed, before popping his door open. I shook my head doing the same. After passing up my father's security, we headed straight to his office. He hated that Khari and I didn't take advantage of all the security, but we liked to live our lives freely without motherfuckas breathing down our backs. The shit was annoying.

Once the double doors were opened for us, my jaw tightened, as I saw that nigga Deon sitting there with his bitch ass daddy, Clayton. I didn't even remember touching that nigga's arms, but he had a cast on, and his face was still bruised with two black eyes and a bandage going across his nose and another on his forehead.

My father was sitting there with a stern look on his face; the same look that he had when I declined the marriage.

"The fuck is this about, baba?" Khari spoke my thoughts. My father huffed at Khari's choice of language, before speaking.

"Apparently, Jahi fought Deon over the prostitute that he acquired from Slim. His father and I are not pleased with your behavior, Jahi, and his father is threatening to back out of our partnership if we don't fix this situation." I looked at my father with a raised eyebrow. He didn't give a fuck about their partnership. Yes, they had influence, but not more than our family. And they were replaceable. My father was attempting to punish me for going against tradition. He was also testing me to see if I valued my relationship with Tove over my family's business and traditions. But he knew it was bullshit when he and my mother had brought that woman there, knowing that I wasn't even supposed to get married for another couple of years or so.

"And how do you suppose we fix it?" I took the seat next to Khari, deciding to let them humor me.

"We would like to buy her from you," Clayton spoke up. "We understand that you lost a great deal of money in that whole ransom situation and assumed that may be why you decided to put your hands on my son when he showed interest in her. Deon told me how pretty and docile she is, and I figured that we could put her to good use." Clayton grinned, and I smiled. He was going to kill Tove to spite me if he got his hands on her.

"How much you talking?" Khari added, as he leaned back into his seat and tugged on his beard, going into bargaining mode.

My father's eyebrows shot up toward his hairline, and Clayton's smile was wiped from his face, as he looked between Khari and I. Deon did what bitches do and started to look uncomfortable and avert his eyes. I wanted to beat his ass again off principle.

"Well, I was thinking that we should settle on a hundred thousand dollars," Clayton quickly recovered, plastering that grin back on.

"And I think that's more than enough for the trouble that she's caused," my father added.

"What do you think, Khari?" I turned to face Khari.

"What do I think? No, what do *you* think? She is your *prostitute,* after all." He shrugged.

"Nah, but you're the better bargainer, so I need to know if you think it's a good deal or not," I exclaimed.

Khari covered his heart with his hand that had a ring on every finger. Khari was extra in every way. "Why thank you, Jahi. I think... that you should go for it." He nodded.

"Okay," I shrugged.

Eyes went back and forth between us and foreheads wrinkled in confusion.

Phew! Phew!

I quickly pulled out my new Beretta with the silencer screwed on and sent a bullet through Deon's head and Clayton's right after.

"Damn, that bitch is smooth," Khari marveled at the gun, as I nodded my agreement with downturned lips.

"So, what you really wanted baba, because I'm off today, and I'd like to spend my day off with my girl." I turned to face my father, and his mouth was hanging open, before he pulled it shut into a tight-lipped grimace. Deon and his father were both slumped in their chairs. They knew better than that. Shit was disrespectful as fuck. I had plans to finish Deon off, but I wanted him to live in fear for a little bit longer.

"I want you to get her the hell out of your house!" he bellowed in that thunderous voice.

"Whew, chile," Khari murmured.

"Don't you see the disrespect that you're showing our family and our tradition behind this woman! I warned you early on, Jahi! I told you not to fall for her, and instead, you disobeyed me! And I had to hear from associates that you bought her a bookstore! What are you doing, Jahi? You have betrayed our family for a woman!"

"Baba, no disrespect, but shut up." My head snapped in Khari's direction. I mean, I did what I wanted to do anyway, but I never just outright disrespected that nigga and told him to shut up.

"What!" he thundered. I don't know if Khari remembered that he was born into an African family, and African families didn't play that disrespect shit.

"You heard me. Shut up! You're the biggest hypocrite of them all. Up here trying to force this man to marry some woman he doesn't know the same way that Babu did you, when you still have your ex around!" he revealed.

"You cheating on mama?" I looked toward my father with knitted brows, as he started to boil over in anger and confusion.

"N-no. No! I would never betray her," he sputtered. "Khari—"

"No. That's enough. Shit. Baba, Jahi does everything that you ask and expect of him. And we all know that when you retire from your position that he'll be the one to pick up where you left off because he's so damned serious. Let him love who he wants to love! It's his life. And stop calling that girl a prostitute because she never was! It's not anybody's business, but Slim kept her hostage. You and mama wearing this arranged marriage mess out. Jahi is in love, Baba. Let him have that!" He was fuming, as he moved his hands all about.

My father's glare wavered from Khari to me, before he sighed, and his countenance softened.

"Is this true, Mkuu? This isn't just about sex, and you are in love with her?"

I gave him a single nod. His eyes roamed to Deon and Clayton, before they came back to me. He waved his hand, and two guards marched from the door to get their bodies.

"Okay." He sighed. "But you better stand on this and your decision to be with her when I take your side in front of the family. And in front of your mother." He pointed at me, as he spoke.

"I appreciate everything that being a part of this family has given me, and no disrespect to the family nor tradition, but I'm marrying her. I'm marrying Tove."

His eyes widened. "So, Mkuu is really in love." A slight grin came to his lips. "I remember that feeling. I've grown to love your mother over the years, but when I met her, I was in love with someone else. Someone from here. I wasn't like you and Khari. You two are so bullheaded, and you don't sway once you've made a decision. And while that is annoying, that is a quality that I can respect and appreciate in the two men that I've raised."

"Thank you." I nodded.

"I guess that I should go prepare your mother for the news of you getting married."

"Sure should, because we're not letting her go anywhere," Khari added.

He nodded, before frowning and asking, "Khari, how did you know about that?"

"I make it my business to know everything about everybody. And when I snooped around in your desk, I saw your picture with her and a letter that she wrote you, before I was born." He shrugged, as if it was no big deal. He had me wondering if he had ever been through my shit before.

Our father sighed, before shocking us and letting out a boisterous laugh. I had to laugh too because Khari just didn't give a fuck. He was always in somebody's business, but that made him a beast at his job.

"So, who's the woman that Baba was in love with?" I asked Khari after we hugged our father and started to leave his office.

"Wouldn't you like to know?" He smirked, before tilting his head in the direction of our father's secretary, Mrs. Melodie. She had been around as long as I could remember, and when I thought about it, it was kind of fucked up that she still worked for him while watching him move on. She had her own family and children that we played with a few times growing up, but now I know that it wasn't her first choice. I knew that my mother didn't care for her, but she never said why. No wonder that nigga was paying her so well and giving her as much vacation time as she wanted, whenever she wanted it. Shit, I'd keep the job too if I was her, considering the benefits.

———

"Tove!" I yelled while jerking the steering wheel to the right because her ass was drifting into the left lane.

"Please remind me why did I get into this car! *Mungu, tafadhli, nisaidie!*" Khari yelled from the backseat, calling out for God's help.

"Because you love me!" Tove shouted, before laughing and pressing her foot on the pedal, going faster.

"Oh, you think this shit is funny?" I frowned, as I looked at her pretty smiling face, before quickly looking back at the road.

"No, y'all just overreacting!"

"Nigga, what?" I spat.

"This bitch has lost her mind. Mkuu, make her pull over!"

"Pull ovaaaaa," Tove mocked Khari, making me chuckle. "Little bitch," she muttered.

I promised Tove that I would teach her how to drive after she asked and gave me big puppy dog eyes. We were on our way to go tiki tubing, and I told her that I would teach her to drive on one of the back roads, since there were hardly any cars or police back there. I regretted my decision the moment I got in the passenger seat, and she turned the key in the ignition. She was driving fast and swerving, and Khari was being tossed from side to side in the backseat, despite wearing a seatbelt.

"This is your stop, Tove!" I yelled, as she rolled her eyes, before pulling to the side of the road and coming to a screeching halt.

"Tove don' got my nuts all twisted up back here. One ball over the other and shit," Khari fussed, as he reached for his crotch.

Tove started laughing until she snorted, which always made me laugh. She got out of the car and swung her head toward the back window, making that big ass bun that sat on top of her head flop to the side. "At least now we know you got some. I just knew you were chafing that coochie the way that you be strutting and walking all hard."

I chortled, as Khari's mouth fell open because she was always on his ass.

"I can't stand your little short ass!" he screamed out the window, before he had to laugh himself.

I took over driving, and I shook my head when Tove pulled a bag of Hot Cheetos from her purse and brought her knees up to her chest. I didn't understand how that was comfortable, but that was her favorite way to sit.

"Want one?" I frowned, as she held that red ass chip up to my lips, making her laugh, before eating it herself.

It wasn't long, before her ass was talking a mile a minute to Khari while trying to feed him Hot Cheetos too. I never knew that so many words could come out of her mouth in a short period of time, since every word was drawled out. I glanced at her and just took a second to take her in. She was definitely worth all of the bullshit with my parents and putting a bullet between Deon and Clayton's eyes. She was worth everything that we went through to get to this moment.

"Baby, shut up," I reached over and ran a hand down her lips, as we pulled up to the camp where we would go tubing, and Khari hopped out to go meet his friends. I started laughing when she frowned at me, curling up her full, mauve-colored upper lip in the process.

"I'mma remember to shut up and keep my mouth closed later too."

"Wait."

"Nah, my lips are sealed." She smirked and hopped out of the car, before I could grab her.

"I didn't mean it like that. I was just playing, baby." I knew I fucked up when I watched her thick hips sway away, as her ass filled out the shorts that she wore over the one-piece swimsuit that looked the same color, as her skin. She was always dressed so simple, but simple shit never looked so sexy. She never had to be extra or revealing. She didn't do anything extra to her hair or nails, except getting her feet done and a clear manicure, and the only time I had ever saw her wear makeup was when I proposed. She was a natural pretty, and she didn't need anything else, which was new for me because I actually liked when bitches got all dressed up and did the most.

"Nope." She threw over her shoulder, before walking to the hut where we were supposed to purchase tubes.

After buying two tubes, since she didn't want to share one with me, and finally getting to the water she was quiet, but her scary ass still waited for me to get in first, before reaching for her and helping her on her tube. She suggested coming here but was terrified that a snake was going to be in the water, and while that was very possible, I wasn't worried about it. Shit usually didn't bother you unless you bothered it.

After floating in silence in the cool water for a while, I tied my tube to hers so that it wouldn't float away, and I propped myself on hers while we floated down the river.

"What? You want to reenact the Titanic. 'Cause I'll push your ass off," she jabbed with those big ass, pink sunglasses on her face and her lips tooted up, as she leaned back in the tube and put her foot on my chest. I looked down at her blue, painted toes.

I chuckled, as I kissed her foot. "You dramatic, as hell. I was just fucking with you because you never used to talk so much. I love hearing you talk though," I admitted, and she blushed.

"You just trying to get some head."

"Unt un."

"Mhmm." She leaned over, and I met her for a kiss on her supple lips.

"Y'all are sickening. Honestly." Khari floated by on a huge yellow tube with his best friend Ashley sitting between his legs, and they had a cooler sitting on another tube that was tied to theirs. Antony and Aniya were already ahead of us on the rocky part where you could stand up and watch the fish swim around your feet.

"And I would swear that y'all are fucking. Honestly." Tove quipped, as she wagged a finger between them. I reached over into their cooler and got her the small bottle of Patrón that Ashley brought for Tove, and I grabbed a water.

"Snake!" Khari yelled, causing Tove to scream and almost flip us off the tube. I was glad that we both could swim because we were past the shallow part, and these waters went deeper than twenty-six feet. Everybody around us started freaking out. People were flipping out of their tubes left and right.

Khari laughed loud as hell, as he and Ashley floated away.

"Baby, there ain't no snake out here," I soothed, as I tried to stifle my laughter because she had buried her face into my chest and wouldn't let me go. The rest of her body was balled up in the tube. I was lying my ass off because I saw one a few moments before Khari yelled it.

"I'm going to kill him," she grumbled against my chest.

"I got you." I moved her from my chest, as I started to kick, so that I could catch up to Khari. He and Ashley were so busy talking that when I got behind him, they weren't paying attention. I pulled the back of his tube down hard as fuck, making him and Ashley flip. I laughed my ass off because all I saw was legs and arms flying, as they tried to get back on their tube.

Tove was snorting and laughing and shit with tears

running down her face, while Khari was cursing and threatening to shoot me.

"I'mma kick yo' asssssss, Mkuu! Tsssss!" he yelled and then hissed, and I chuckled when Tove wagged her tongue at him while holding up her middle finger. "And I'm going to hold your big ass head underwater, Tove!" We laughed harder, as we started to float ahead of them.

They were climbing back on, and I felt a little bad for Ashley when I saw her hair all fucked up with her puff all lopsided, but I shrugged it off. She was a casualty. Nobody fucked with my baby and got away with it.

When Tove finally stopped laughing, she leaned forward to kiss me with a bright smile on her face. *Yeah*, she was worth everything that we went through to get to this moment.

"So, now I can get head when we get home?"

She tittered, before nodding and leaning in for another kiss. "Yup."

Chapter Thirteen

TOVE

"The most dangerous creation of any society is the man who has nothing to lose."

"Oh, wow that's some heavy literature you're reading there."

My eyes roamed from the pages of James Baldwin's *The Fire Next Time* and up to the face of a woman with pale, fawn-colored skin, a round face, dark brown hair, and dark brown eyes. She looked to be in her late forties.

"To some, it may seem heavy. Especially if you can't even begin to conceptualize the grievances of being African American in the United States. To me, it's a cultural work of art." I leaned across the smoothed white oak countertop, placing a fist under my chin, and placing the book face down.

Her eyes widened, and I could tell that I had made her

uncomfortable. My eyes roamed to Daniel, who stood at the counter of the cafe with a smirk on his face, as he looked on in amusement.

"Welcome to *Cover Cove*. How can I help you?" I plastered a smile on my face. She chuckled and then sighed, as if my fake smile had made her feel relieved.

"Well, I'm the one who called for the first edition of Alice in Wonderland and bid over the phone." She smiled like a child waiting for a golden sticker. I remembered loosely what she was talking about because Khari mentioned taking the bid, but I wasn't there anymore at that point.

"Okay, great. What's your name and confirmation number?" I lifted from my resting spot on the counter and grabbed the notepad and pen, so that I could go retrieve her order and make sure that the names and confirmation numbers matched.

"Coral Monroe."

My eyes roamed back up to her face from the pad, before I could start to write. I didn't know much about my family from the bayou since we had moved when I was very young. I knew that the last name Monroe was pretty common around here, but I was just so curious.

"You wouldn't just so happen to be from Delacroix or anywhere around there, huh?"

"Oh, me? No." She giggled. "My husband is though. Do you know anyone from there?" she asked. I shook my head because her husband wasn't present, so it wasn't like I could ask him anything. She looked confused, as I started to write her name and confirmation number down on the notepad.

"Okay, I'm going to go and grab that for you."

I grabbed my keys to the storage room, and this time, I locked the door behind me. I knew Deon had gotten his ass whipped, but I didn't want people to make it a habit of walking up on me.

After grabbing the book and placing in into the air-tight glass casing and locking it, I placed the key to the casing in a golden-toned, tiny, cloth bag and placed both into a *Cover Cove* shopping bag with tissue paper. I also added an instruction manual on how to handle first edition books or any older books that you wanted to preserve.

"Alright. So, I included an instruction manual on preservation, and the key is in the gold bag," I instructed, as I placed her bag onto the counter. A bright smile spread from cheek to cheek across her face.

"Oh my gosh, I can't wait to—"

"Did you finally get it, honey?" I heard a man's voice, as he walked into the store, and both my and her eyes flew to him.

"Yes! And it's perfect!" she all but screamed, but he couldn't respond because his eyes were locked on me. My eyes roamed over his face, and he had gotten older. His dark, short beard and hair had started to gray. He was bigger and healthy-looking, and his hair was cut shorter than I remembered, but you could still see that wavy pattern. His pale skin was even all over, with only his rosy cheeks being colored. He looked happy. He looked whole. He looked *alive*. And he looked clean; albeit I didn't know that he was using when I was younger either.

"Is... everything alright?" Coral asked, as her head turned between he and I. Our identical green eyes pierced into one another's.

"Daddy?" I croaked out, as my throat burned from me trying to hold back my cries.

"Excuse me?" Coral's face washed over in confusion, and he couldn't move just like I couldn't.

"Coral, let's go," he instructed, making my eyes grow large.

"Daddy!" I screamed, alarming everyone in the store.

"Mark, you told me that your daughter was dead. That she had died with your ex-wife!"

"You told her that I was dead, daddy?" I asked with my eyes frantically moving between him and her, as I walked from behind the counter toward him.

"Slim told me that you were dead!" I pointed at him for emphasis.

"Coral!" he screamed her name, making her flinch and grab her bag.

"Daddy, wait! Please talk to me! You owe me that much!" I yelled at the top of my lungs. At this point, Daniel had come from his place behind the counter and came to my side.

"Tove, everyone is looking at you," he whispered in my ear, but I jerked away from him. I didn't give a fuck who was watching.

"Mark, what is going on?" Coral questioned hesitantly, as he snatched her hand and started to pull her out of the store.

"Nothing! I don't know her! She's crazy!"

"I'm crazy? I'm crazy!" I bellowed, as I followed them out of the store onto the sidewalk. I saw Craig approach me from the corner of my eye. He stuck around when I was at the store without Jahi, to protect me, since we didn't know where Slim was.

Coral turned to look at me with frantic eyes, as he kept pulling her, but I grabbed onto his shirttail and pulled at it. I briefly wondered was he denying me because I was black, but that couldn't have been the case. He had walked around with a black daughter by his side for sixteen years and a black wife for even longer.

"Talk to me!" I screamed in his face. He shoved at my hands, but I wasn't letting go.

"Please talk to me." I felt the warm tears rushing down my face like water rushed down a river bend. "Please tell me why!" I pleaded with him. He couldn't even look me in the eyes.

"Tell you why what? Tell her why what?" Coral queried.

"Nothing. She's crazy! Can anybody help me!" he screamed with his face balled up and beet red, making me grow infuriated. How did he even muster up the audacity to be upset?

"Tell me why you sold me for drugs! Tell me why you didn't come back for me once you were clean! Tell me why you didn't love me! Tell me what I ever did to you to deserve that?" I sobbed while yanking at his shirt while he continued to pull away from me. Coral's eyes widened, and she yanked her hand away from his.

He finally raised his head to look me in my eyes, but he raised his fist, as well to hit me. Before he could strike me, Craig had lifted my feet from the ground and pried my hands away from his shirt. I shook violently, as I cried, and Craig carried me to the truck.

"I'm sorry, Tove. Some people just real fucked up, baby girl," he muttered, before shutting the back door to the truck. I quickly looked behind me and saw that just like that, he and Coral had disappeared. I was upset that Coral didn't try to do more, but I let that feeling go as soon as it came because she didn't owe me anything, he did.

"Why?" I laid on the backseat and sobbed. "Why! Why! Why! Why!" I punched the seat every time that I spoke. My heart was obliterated. He was fine and healthy and had moved on with his life and left me behind. He left me with Slim to be tortured, and he told his wife that I was dead. Did he have a fake grave for me, as well? What the fuck could I make of this? I couldn't blame drugs or him being sick.

"Tove," Craig spoke softly, as he turned around and looked at me with those sympathetic eyes. I turned my back to him and faced the seat, before I heard him sigh. I was inconsolable.

I heard him mumbling something, and I assumed that he was on the phone with Jahi.

"Tove, you're home," he said softly, as I peeled my eyes open. I had cried so hard, that I started to fall asleep on the way home. I slowly sat up, before looking down and noticing that my purse was beside me. I didn't know when Craig had gotten it or placed it by me. After putting it on my shoulder, Craig opened the door, and I hopped out, and there he was, waiting for me by the door. He didn't give me sad eyes; his expression was unreadable, just like it was the night that he had turned into someone else and beat the shit out of Deon.

My eyes began to well again, and my lips quivered, before I ran toward him and jumped into his arms. I let everything out, as my body shivered.

"Thank you," I mouthed to Craig over Jahi's shoulder, as he gave me a single nod. I didn't want him to think that I didn't appreciate him. After all, he knew just who I needed.

"Let it out," Jahi spoke into my ear lowly, as I cried, and his large hand brushed up and down my back. He carried me into the house and up the three flights of stairs. "I'm so sorry, baby."

For some reason, being consoled made me cry harder. He tried to lay me on the plush, stark white comforter, but I wouldn't let go of his neck. I pulled back a little and looked into his eyes, and his eyes briefly roamed my face, before he nodded. He knew exactly what I was asking for. I didn't want to use my words to express my pain. My words had never really worked for me anyway. I wanted to speak to him in that language that only we knew. That language that transferred our energy to one another.

I watched, as he pulled away from me, this time I let him go, and he began to shed his shirt, shorts and then boxers. He stalked toward me, as our eyes locked, before he started to undress me. Sneakers. Jeans. Panties. Oversized black t-shirt that I stole from him. Bra. My crying had slowed down to low whimpers and my tears no longer rushed in rivers down my face.

"I love you," he told me, as he looked into my eyes. He didn't give me a chance to return the sentiments, before his lips latched onto mine, so I decided to let him feel my love. He looked shocked when I leaned forward and stood up to push him on the bed. He sat up on his elbows and looked at me with his brows knitting together, before I grabbed him and slid down his girthy, long dick. I watched, as his face contorted in pleasure, as he loudly called my name, before my head fell back in pleasure. I almost came just from the way that he filled me up.

Once I recovered, I began to bounce on him, and he gripped my hips, before thrusting upward into me. I wanted it rough, and I guess that my body language conveyed that since he delivered powerful stroke after powerful stroke. He started speaking all kind of Swahili words to me that I didn't understand. And I didn't need to understand them because I understood our dialect. I didn't shed another tear until it was from 8.9 Jahi, causing that eruption from within me. By the way he tended to my body, and looked into my eyes as much as possible, I knew that he felt the pain that I was trying to nonverbally convey. I was relieved that he understood because how could I explain or say what I didn't know? My daddy had literally given me nothing and betrayed me again. I would've rather kept him dead and believed that he wasn't in his right mind.

After Jahi and I shared another earth-shattering orgasm, I began to sob all over again while he was still buried deep inside of me. I covered my face, as he held me and let me get it all out. He didn't even have to speak because his presence was more than enough; it always had been. I hated that I was so fragile behind someone that had already erased me from their memory and their life. I made a mental note to myself that this would be the last time that I cried behind my daddy and this situation.

Chapter Fourteen

JAHI

"Rougarou or *Loup Garou*. You can use either or," Tove spoke, as she swiped her greasy fingers over my left peck and over the tattoo of a menacing wolf. She quickly used the back of her hand to attempt to wipe the grease away.

"So, that means wolf?" I asked, as my index finger drew infinity symbols across the supple skin on her calf. I was sitting between her thick, soft legs on the bedroom floor, as she sat on an ottoman and scalp braided my hair after doing her own. I thought it was weird as fuck when couples did that matching shit, but she insisted, and I'd do anything to make her feel better after her encounter with her bitch ass daddy. She wouldn't talk about it, but Craig gave me the gist of how things went awry.

"Nah, well, a werewolf. It's basically the swamp monster of

the bayou. Had me scared shitless when I was little." Her sultry voice vibrated in my ears, since I was so tall that I was close to her mouth, even sitting on the floor. She chuckled, making me do the same. She was teaching me a few Cajun-French words, per my request. She said she didn't know much but would teach me what she could remember. I loved to hear her talk and hearing her speak in the broken French just made her thick accent all the better.

"What was it like for you in the bayou? Do you have any other family?" I pried. I wanted to know why no one was looking for her after all of that time.

My finger stopped moving across her skin when I felt her rough ass hands stop tugging at my scalp.

"Nah. Well..." she paused. I was about to tell her don't worry about it until she started to speak again, and her hands started to pull at my scalp. "I honestly don't know if anyone is still alive or anything. From five 'til I was fourteen, it was always my daddy, ma, and me. My family in the bayou didn't want nothing to do with my ma or daddy."

My jaw tightened, as she started a new braid and gripped the front of my hair tighter. I wasn't going to have a hairline fucking with her.

"Why not? Because they weren't the same race?"

"Nah. My daddy's brother shot my ma's brother over a dice game. He got mad 'cause my uncle took all of his money. He tried to get it back by playing his car but lost that too. He couldn't fight for shit, so he got his ass whipped, and after that, he came back with a gun." She chuckled, but I found the family history disturbing and fucked up. But I guess when you've been through a lot of shit, you laughed to cover the pain and to deal with it.

She continued, "And that caused a family beef, but my ma and daddy were already in love, and I was five years old, so they chose to stay together. That shit got them run out of the bayou by my daddy's family, even though it was my uncle on that side's fault. You know how white people can be though."

I absentmindedly nodded out of habit, making her pull at my scalp tighter. I gripped her calf. "Baby, are you mad at a nigga or something? Damn. I'm about to be around this bitch with my hairline in the middle of my head like Stevie Wonder, but I won't be too blind to see it."

I felt her double over against my back, as her body shook and she started to laugh and snort, of course. I couldn't help but chuckle with her after that.

"Alright. Sorry. I forgot that you was a pussy," she spoke with laughter laced in her tone.

"Ah!" she screamed, before she started laughing when I turned around and yanked her on the floor with me and started to wrestle with her.

When I finally let her go, she kept laughing until tears came to her eyes, before she quieted down, and we just laid on the floor and stared into one another's eyes. I found myself getting lost in her eyes often, at random moments.

"Don't kill him, Jahi."

"What?" My face balled up, as if I was confused, but I knew exactly what she was talking about. Tove was learning me. She never saw me kill anyone before, but somehow, she knew my plans. I was going to kill his ass tonight. Not only did he fuck her over, but he also humiliated her and raised his fist to hit her, and if Craig wasn't there, then he would've.

"Don't kill my daddy." She looked at me with dead eyes that glazed over, as she blinked. I could tell that she was trying to put back up that mental barrier that she had up to protect her mind from him. She was trying to numb herself.

My jaw tightened because he had fucked her over time and time again, yet she was still trying to be gracious and save him.

"Okay."

"Jahi—"

"I said, *okay*," I told her, as she just stared at me for a moment longer, before getting up. I watched, as she took her seat back on the ottoman, before waving for me to come back. I sighed, before sitting back up.

"That shit ain't funny, Tove." I winced, as she started tugging on my scalp again, and her ass was chortling.

"Hey, don't they speak French in Africa?" she asked once she settled down.

"Yeah, in some parts. But my family only speaks the official languages of Tanzania; English and Swahili. Also, the French isn't the same. Cajun-French is patois."

"Oh, right. *Defunt*," she continued in the broken language.

"*Defunt?*"

"Mhm. Means dead. Like... my ma would be *defunt* Belle. So, dead Belle."

"Damn. That shit sounds morbid," I mused aloud, as my finger started to draw infinity symbols again. She chuckled.

"Nah. It's actually meant respectfully," she said, as I absentmindedly nodded again, and she yanked at my hair again.

"Tove!" I shouted, and she laid her weight against my back and started laughing again. Her ass was goofy as hell, but it was good to know that I could make her laugh. I thought more on her request and let it roll over in my mind. I was trying to weigh my options, as I wondered would I be hurting her more. It felt like every time that I got her to open up more, she was hit with some other bullshit. It wasn't in my nature to just not do anything when I had killed for way... *way* less. Especially when I would do anything for my heart.

I couldn't do it. I tried to lay in bed with Tove and listen to her request, but I couldn't. My eyes steadied on the staggered rise and fall of her chest, as she breathed heavily in her sleep. Her hair was tied up in one of my durags, and that shit made me chuckle because she was always wearing my shit. Her little ass even had on my boxers and t-shirt.

It was in that moment that I for sure decided that I couldn't let him live his life knowing that he had fucked over her. Even though life had hardened her to a certain extent, there was still an innocence there.

I slowly pulled my arm from under her and watched for a while until she turned her back to me and buried herself further under the covers. I dipped into my closet, before throwing on some black joggers, a hoodie, and all black Jordans that I kept just for murking season. I grabbed my new favorite Beretta, before heading out of the closet to make sure that she was still asleep.

My mind raced, as I drove to the location that I had gotten on him and his wife. His bitch ass did one thing right and ain't have no more kids after Tove. My fist gripped the wheel tighter, as I floated in between cars. I was on a fucking mission, and when I got like this, not much could bring me down besides her. It was Tove that made me calm down sooner than I normally would have that night that I beat Deon's ass. If she wasn't there, he definitely would've died that night. She was attentive to me, even though I could tell that she was scared at first. That shit fucked with my head a little because she was the only person that I didn't want to feel that way about me. Everybody else, I didn't care.

I checked my gun and twisted on the silencer once I pulled up and parked on the street beside the house. They lived in a quiet, decent neighborhood where there was a good amount of space in between the houses, and that was going to work in my favor. I crept up to the decent-sized brick house, and I noticed that the garage was open, and one of the cars registered to them wasn't there. Khari pulled all of that shit, cars, houses, bank accounts, he had accessed it all. Mark had gotten him a nice little job as a stockbroker after he got out of rehab six years ago. This motherfucka been clean for six of the seven years that Tove was with Slim, and he still left her with him. He had married his wife fresh out of rehab.

I smirked when I attempted to disable the alarm, but it was already unarmed. This was about to be easy. I used a lock-pick and quickly unlocked the door. It was then that I heard low, country music. I followed the sound of the music, and it led me to the backyard. I opened the door, and we instantly locked eyes when he turned around from his spot in the white lawn chair. This bitch was denying Tove, and she had his whole fucking face. He looked shocked, as his eyes roamed to my hand that gripped my Beretta tightly. I was ready to send his ass to Hell.

"You're here about her, huh? I knew it was going to be some shit when that bodyguard looking motherfucka carried her away," he slurred with his face relaxing, before he turned around and took a swig of his beer. He was drunk; albeit, I could still hear the thick drawl with every word he spoke. It was then that I took notice that it must've been his wife who had left in the car. Good for her, because she was going to have to be a casualty if she was here. No life, no witness. I lived by that shit.

I said nothing, as he continued to speak. "She always had that effect on people. Everybody always loved her and wanted to be around her. When she started high school, I damn near had to beat 'em off with a bat." He chuckled, before taking another swig.

"I'm not here to collect on an autobiography or memoir. You fucked up, my guy." I stepped closer and closed the door behind me. I appreciated the fact that the backyard was closed off with a wooden gate.

His head switched back around to me. "Can I at least finish my beer first?" he asked seriously. I wanted to go ahead and kill him, but I decided against it. I had some questions to see if there was anything that I could offer Tove.

I gave him a single nod, and he turned back around to face nothing in particular.

"My wife left me. When we got home, she demanded that I tell her everything or she'd leave, so I told her, and she still fucking left me."

I stalked toward him, before taking the seat next to him. I guess he thought that I was supposed to feel sorry for him, but I didn't.

"Can you tell me what would make a man sell his daughter for drugs?" I got straight to the point. He was quiet, with only the sounds of the music being heard until I took my gun off safety. I wasn't playing with him. I didn't play with my prey.

"Shit, it ain't nothing you'll like." He shrugged, countenance careless, before he continued. "She looks just like her mother to me. I started doing the shit because her mother died, and there I was, with a constant reminder every day. Eventually, I had run out of money, and I had nothing but me, a house that I was about to lose, and her. I wasn't going to be able to take care of her anyway." He shrugged again, before taking another swig. I didn't even know why the fuck I entertained him. There was never going to be any reason good enough to give Tove or anything that he could say to satisfy her because the shit just didn't make sense. He was a bitch, and that was all there was to it. It took everything in me to not beat his ass to death.

"I'm done," he said, before setting the empty bottle on the ground beside his feet and sitting back in the chair and closing his eyes. I just looked at him for a moment and tried to calm myself down. I realized then that he was the type that couldn't live without a woman. At first, he turned to cocaine, and now he was back here getting drunk.

"You ever heard of poetic justice?"

"What?" His face balled up, as he opened his eyes to look at me. I relaxed in the chair and set the gun in my lap.

"The textbook definition is 'the fact of experiencing a fitting or deserved retribution for one's actions'," I schooled. "You see, because killing you while you're miserable seems too good for a piece of shit like you. That's a mercy killing, and I don't do that shit. I like to look a motherfucka in his eyes while he's scared for his life and begging, before I kill his ass. And that ain't you right now. So, I'm going to keep an eye on you and wait until you get happy. I mean until you're on top of the fucking world. I'm going to wait until you're as happy as a man doing his first line of coke and feeling nothing but that first high euphoria. I mean, I just can't wait until you and your wife either patch shit up or you move on." I gave him a tight smile that made his eyebrows tent.

"And just when you're at the happiest moment of your fucking life, I'll be here to kill whoever it is that you care about right in front of you. More than that, I'll be your personal fucking reaper and send your ass straight to the pits of Hell." I spoke with venom laced in my tone, before rising from the seat. He looked at me with saddened eyes like he was upset that he wasn't getting his mercy kill. "Oh, and don't try to make amends with Tove once you get your shit together. We are *way* past that. Also, you can count that, as your last beer. I'll have somebody watching you to make sure you never drink or do another drug again. We're going to dry yo' bitch ass out. You also can't leave town, and I got the power to make all this shit happen.

"You don't deserve to be able to cope with the shit that you've done nor losing your wife because of it. Enjoy your life, Mark. Get happy." I chuckled and patted his shoulder, before walking back inside the house so that I could leave. I heard his ass start crying behind me, but it didn't stop my stride. He didn't have a fuck to give when my baby was crying out to him. Either I was going to body his ass, or he was going to body himself out of misery. And I had a gut feeling that he was too pussy to do the latter.

When I got back into my car, I stretched my hand and realized that I was gripping my gun tight as fuck. It took everything in me not to kill him, but he didn't deserve to die just yet. He didn't deserve anything but that same heartbreak and misery that he gave to Tove.

. . .

Once I was back home, I sat in my car for a moment and shot off a text to the person that I'd have watching Mark to make sure he didn't purchase any drugs nor alcohol.

When I walked back into the bedroom, I froze, as I saw Tove's eyes flow from the TV to me. Her ass had that shit on the lowest volume that it could go like she was listening for me. She sat there, stirring something in a cup while sitting there with her legs crossed. We had a stare off for a moment, before her eyes flowed back to the TV. That was one thing about Tove. Unless you tried to talk to her and she ignored you, you didn't really know if she was mad or not. Her face was pretty much the same all the time, unless she was talking or laughing.

I took that as an opportunity to dip into my closet and change into just my boxers. I came out of the closet and climbed into the bed with her, and she still wasn't saying anything. She was just sitting there eating something out of a cup and watching TV. I wrapped my arm around her waist and laid my head on the pillow beside her.

"Did you kill him?" she asked after a while.

"No."

"Was he somehow dead when you left the house?"

I chuckled at her asking me the same question but in a different way, before saying, "No."

"Will he die?"

"We all will someday," I replied. I would never admit to killing anyone except Slim, to her. He was at the top of my shit list, and she knew that, so there was no sense in hiding that.

It wasn't that I didn't trust her, I just didn't want her to fully know that side of me. I didn't want her to know that I was a straight up killer and that I was perfectly fine with that.

She must've been satisfied because she didn't ask me anything else. I lifted my head to see what she was smacking on.

"What the fuck is that?" I frowned, making her eyes roam my face, before she grinned.

"Beanie weenies."

"What the fuck is that?" I repeated.

"Beans and fucking weenies."

I raised an eyebrow at her smart-ass mouth, before looking in her cup. "Shit looks gross. When the fuck that got in our kitchen?"

"When Barika made the grocery list, and I added it on there," she quipped, eyes now back watching *Love and Hip-Hop Atlanta.* "And it's not gross. Yo' ass just don't know nothing about a struggle meal."

"And you ain't about to make my ass feel bad about that either. I never ate a hot dog in my life."

"Khari has," she chortled, making me frown. "Taste it." She quickly stretched the spoon into my face, making me flinch.

"Hell no." I frowned.

"It's good. Just taste it." Her voice softened, and she did that puppy shit with her eyes.

"First Hot Cheetos, now this shit," I groused, before leaning forward and taking a bite. I was shocked 'cause the shit was lowkey good. I didn't even have to say shit because a grin spread across her pretty face.

"See, this not regular beenie weenies. I sautéed onions first and put a little season salt, a dash of sugar and onion powder in here like my ma used to do," she spoke with a finger pointing into the bowl.

"I can't really tell. Let me taste it again and see," I lied. Her lips tooted to the side like she didn't believe me, but she still gave me some more, and the shit was actually good. I wouldn't eat it every day because I didn't eat anything from a can, but I'd eat this sometimes with her. I just looked at her and shook my head while she watched TV and ate, every other bite, stretching her spoon my way to share. She really came in my life and started changing shit. Her presence was gentle yet a force to be reckoned with—even in silence. I thought briefly to the meaning of her name, and she *was* the human form of beautiful thunder.

"Tove, you have to take this out of my head. I can't sleep with my dreams being yanked from my fucking brain," I told her once we got back in the bed after brushing our teeth and she cut the TV off. I was trying to get comfortable, but there wasn't nothing but pressure on my head every time that I tried to really relax. Her body shook against my chest, as she laughed at me and buried her face further into my chest. It wasn't until she started snorting did I laugh. I could do this goofy shit with her forever.

Chapter Fifteen
TOVE

"You ready?"

"Nope," I answered honestly, making Khari break out into a cackle. We had just pulled up to the house that I used to live in with Slim and the other girls, and I was not ready to go back inside of there. I knew he told me that someone else had taken over, but there wasn't anything in there for me but bad vibes, bad memories, and bitches that hated me for no apparent reason.

"You gon' be fine. Let me check you out." His eyes ran over me from the tight knot he made me put my hair into, the thin layer of Vaseline on my face, then to the black Nike sports bra that I wore with the matching leggings, and then he frowned when he leaned over and looked at my feet.

"What?" I asked with my eyes following his line of vision to look at the all-black shoes that I had on.

"What the fuck are *those*? Tove, I told you to put on shoes."

"These *are* shoes," I stressed with my hands pointed at my feet. Khari was already shaking his head, and I was thoroughly confused.

"Where the fuck did you get them from?"

"Walmart."

"*Walmart?*" he snarled. "When the fuck did you go to Walmart? What would you need from a Walmart?" he fired off question after question.

"I had Craig to take me after work. And since you, Jahi, and Barika buy me literally everything, I didn't necessarily *need* anything. I just wanted to walk around and check out some stuff, and then I found these and a few puzzles. What's the big deal? I like them." I frowned, as I tilted my left foot to the side to inspect the shoe.

"You wanted to walk around at Walmart?" He scrutinized me with his face balled up like he had a nasty taste in his mouth.

"Yes! Khari! At *Walmart!*" I fussed, growing agitated.

"Okay, bitch, pump the breaks. Save all that animosity for them bitches that beat yo' ass," he snapped, reminding me of the reason that we were here. "All that mouth and no hands. Tsssss." He hissed, before swinging his door open. "Aht! Don't you touch that door!" he fussed, as he saw me about to open my own door. You would swear that I was made out of porcelain by the way that he and Jahi acted sometimes.

"Come on with yo' fucking beat-a-bitch eighteens on. Tove, only criminals wear shoes like that and bitches with small ponytails that can fight. And then here you go. Neither."

I narrowed my eyes at him, as he talked about my ass like a dog.

"Bitch, you better be able to do something other than that eye shit with them shoes on. What kind of shoes are they? What kind of shoes do they even sell at *Walmart*? That's them shoes that the niggas fresh out of jail get when they in the halfway house and they about to start their first shift at McDonald's. Tell me something, Tove, are those slip-resistant? Because that's the only reason that I can see you needing them, so you don't fall while getting beat up."

I just stood there with my arms across my chest and stared at him because I really hated him right now. He didn't have to say all of that.

"Oh, and don't forget this." He ignored my glare, as he reached into the backseat of the convertible and grabbed the metal Louisville Slugger.

"You think that this is fair, though?" I frowned, grabbing the bat with two hands.

"Bitch they slung you down some stairs and jumped you, don't you?"

I nodded, thinking that he had a point.

"Now, march!" He spun me around by my shoulders and smacked me on the ass. I rolled my eyes and treaded to the door slowly and nervously. I wasn't going to lie and say that I wasn't scared when I was. They fucked me up the first time, and I was just going to let it go, but Khari and Jahi didn't believe in stuff like that. They were strong believers in Newton's third law that 'for every action, there is an equal and opposite reaction'. But Jahi was out of town and didn't know what we were up to right now.

When we got to the door, Khari stood in front of me, and he didn't even have to knock, before the door was swung open.

"What's up, Mr. Nuru?" I heard a gruff voice ask, and that just made my punk ass more scared.

"They ready?"

"Yup. Upstairs in the first bedroom to the right. They think they're having a threesome, just like you requested. I don't know why because I took them old, stale pussy hoes off rotation 'bout a month ago."

That made me stifle a snicker.

I watched, as Khari bobbed his head, and then I saw a tall, cocky, dark-skinned man with a bald head lean to look at me behind him.

"Jahi," Khari said with a thumb pointed over his shoulder at me, and, as if that was a command, the man instantly stood upright and walked away from the door.

"What the hell was that?" I asked.

"Never you mind. Bring ya ass." He grabbed my hand and pulled me with him to the stairwell, and I glanced at the man to see that he had completely turned his back to us.

Once we got to the door, I noticed that my hands were sweaty, as I gripped onto the bat. Khari turned to face me and looked me up and down again, before nodding his approval until he got to the shoes and frowned. He shoved me beside the door, before he pushed it open.

"Damn, you fine! I thought you were the gay one though?" I heard Lani's voice followed by giggles and immediately rolled my eyes. From what I recognized through brief encounters, she was always the pack leader, and everyone else was like her little goons, so she was the most vocal. I watched, as Khari raised an eyebrow, before he sauntered into the room. "I—I didn't mean anything by that though, Mr. Nuru," she stuttered.

"Tove!" Khari called my name.

"Huh?" Lani asked, sounding nervous.

I closed my eyes and took a deep breath, before opening them and putting on my game face. I wasn't about to let them feel like they placed fear in my heart. I swung around the corner while twirling the bat.

"What the fuck?" was all that she could mutter, before Khari pulled her up from her place on the bed, next to the other two girls that jumped me, and tossed her my way.

Crack!

I panicked and just swung the bat as fast and hard, as I could. Lani's body hit the ground in a heap, as blood poured from her face and the other two girls screamed. I didn't even know where the blood was coming from.

"Is-is she dead?" I panicked, as I started to hyperventilate.

"Doesn't matter. Who's next?" Khari shrugged, before wagging a finger between the two chicks sitting on the bed. I looked up, and their eyes were as wide, as mine, as they looked down at Lani's body.

"Which one of y'all bitches jumped in second after the mouthy one?" he asked while crossing his arms. They both pointed the finger at the other. "Hmm. I'mma go with you since you need that fucked up wig peeled back anyway." He lucked up and grabbed the second girl, who jumped in by her hair, and immediately, her lace front ripped up in the front. I winced, as she yelped out in pain, as some of her hair came up with the wig.

"Wait!" she screamed, as my eyes snapped shut, and I swung as hard as I could again, making her fall on top of Lani.

"Shit!" I made a mistake by dropping the bat, and that gave the third girl the opportunity to hop from her place on the bed and run toward me swinging. I panicked and just started windmilling on her ass.

"Come on, Tove! Put those prison-system 2000s to work!" Khari yelled.

She got in some good licks in my face, but they kind of just slid off because of the Vaseline. When she hit me in my jaw really hard, I got angry, and I lifted my leg and donkey kicked her ass into the wall, making her fall back. And that gave me the opportunity to sit on her and deliver blow after blow to her face while her arms were at her sides under my legs.

The memories of that night that they jumped me just

started to flood in, and I grabbed her head and repeatedly slammed it onto the marble floors, not even stopping once I saw blood. Eventually, I felt Khari bring a strong arm around my waist and pull me off of her. I looked down at her, and she was laying there knocked out with her head leaking.

My chest heaved up and down, as Khari carried me out of the room, hanging over his arm like a rag doll. I heard him tell the gruff-voiced man something about being good on taxes next month and having a mess to clean up, before he carried me out the door. Once we stepped outside, he placed me on my feet.

"You good?" he asked, as he gripped my jaw and inspected my face.

I nodded, chest still heaving up and down. I still felt rage and adrenalin surging through me.

"Not a scratch." He raised an eyebrow and nodded appreciatively.

"Did I... did I kill them?" I asked, as my rage started to settle, but my chest still heaved.

"No."

"Khari—"

"No," he told me again, looking me directly in my eyes, as I searched his face to see if he was lying. I couldn't tell. He and Jahi could be so unreadable at times.

Once back in the car, I was quiet, as I thought about Lani and how fucked up she had been to me in the past. I decided that I wouldn't worry about what happened to her because she didn't give a fuck about me and was glad that I took her place.

"Tove."

"I'm good," I told Khari, already knowing that he was about to ask.

"I wasn't about to ask that. I know you're good. You're always going to be good when you're with me. I was just about to say that I needed to get some of those Hit-a-Lick 800s 'cause you fucked some shit up in those. Baby, you didn't slip or nothing. At first, I was nervous when you dropped that bat, but when you lifted that thunder thigh and kicked that bitch with them roach-stomper twenties, I knew you were good."

I glanced at him and tried to frown but broke out into a grin, before we started to chortle.

"I can't stand your ass," I said, before bursting out into full-on laughter.

———

After Khari dropped me back off to the house, I took a shower, took down my hair, and quickly threw on some clothes, so that I could go to the bookstore. I had to get there to sell a first edition, and I was the only one that handled those transactions.

"Whoa, lil' bit, what you got on? I think you better take your lil' ass in that house and change." Craig pointed at the house behind me and frowned, as I looked down at myself. I thought that I looked cute in the blue sports bra and bike tights set with the white version of the shoes that I had on earlier.

"I think I look okay."

"Jahi not gon' think that," he quipped while shaking his head.

"Jahi ain't here, and I'm sure he won't mind. Come on, I gotta get to the store," I waved him off, before opening the door myself and hopping in the back seat. Jahi offered to buy me a car, but I actually liked Craig's company and when he took me places.

He got in the truck and looked back at me, before huffing and shaking his head. "Jahi gon' kill my ass," he muttered, but I just shook my head and enjoyed the ride. I started telling Craig about my day, but I couldn't tell if he was listening or not because he wasn't responding. Jahi could be scary, but he wasn't that bad. He literally had grown men worried about how he would react.

"Thanks, Craig." I hopped out of the back seat, as he grunted while holding the door open for me.

I shrugged, before walking in the store. I looked around, and I saw Daniel servicing a long line of people at the cafe. I swear some people just came for the coffee, but it didn't matter because all of the money came to the same place. I walked into my office, and I saw that I still had about thirty minutes before the customer came to pick up their book, so I sat on my desk and crossed my legs, deciding to work on a puzzle.

"Come in!" I called out when I heard a tap on the door.

"Shit," Daniel hissed, as his eyes ran up and down my body. I tilted my head with my eyebrows raised, making his eyes flow to my face. "Oh, shit. My bad, boss lady. I just came to bring you some hot cocoa." He held up the cup, as he tried to keep his eyes on my face.

"Oh, thanks." I held my hand out for it. He made the best cocoa and made a habit of bringing me a cup every day that we both were here. He treaded over to me and handed me the cup, and I grabbed it, before taking a sip and putting my eyes back on my puzzle.

"What you got there?"

"A crossword puzzle. It's surprisingly stumping me."

"Lemme see. I'm actually good at those." He leaned over closer to me, allowing me to catch a whiff of his gentle but pleasant-smelling cologne. "They come in last... hmm. The answer is XYZ."

My head snapped in his direction, before I shoved him, making him break out into a cute grin. "Daniel! I've been trying to figure this out for the past two days!" I felt dumb, and he just chuckled. I made a mistake and dropped the puzzle to the ground, and I let my legs down to pick it up, but Daniel was already grabbing it. When he came up, he came to stand between my thighs and stared into my eyes. I instantly felt uncomfortable or like I was cheating on Jahi.

"Can I take you out, Tove?" he asked, as he held back the puzzle from my reach when I reached for it. He looked at me with hopeful eyes while wearing a cute smirk, and I kind of felt bad for him. The store had been so busy that I never got to tell him that Jahi and I made up.

"Can he take you out, Tove?" I heard Jahi's voice, as he appeared in the doorway. I could've died at that moment, and I'm sure all of the color drained from my face. This looked really bad for Daniel to be standing in front of me, while I sat on this desk and we were in my office alone.

Daniel turned around. "Oh, what's up?" he spoke to Jahi, but Jahi didn't acknowledge him. His eyes were hard on me, as they looked me up and down, and his jaw tightened.

"Daniel, I'm engaged," I mumbled.

"Oh. Oh, okay." He nodded with disappointment etched across his face, before placing the puzzle beside me on the desk.

"Nigga, you gon' step the fuck back out her face or I'mma have to make you?" some version of Jahi thundered, making me close my eyes and take a deep breath. Maybe I would call this version of him Hulk.

"Nah, you good," Daniel spoke up, and I opened my eyes to see his hands up in surrender, as he walked out of the room past a fuming Jahi. I knew that he didn't want to deal with Jahi's crazy ass, and I wouldn't either if I was him. Jahi towered over Daniel and was way bigger than Daniel's lanky frame.

"Jahi—"

"What the fuck you got going on, Tove? You wearing this shit here and this nigga in your face? This how you do shit when I'm out of town? And where the fuck is your ring?" He was walking into the room and shutting the door behind him now. My right hand flew over my left that still held the cocoa, and I realized that I never put my ring back on after earlier.

"This is just something I threw on to get here in time—"

"Oh, it looks like you got plenty of fucking time to me!" he spat.

"I meant to put my ring back on, but I forgot after I was with Khari," I tried to explain, as he walked up on me. I quickly put the cup aside, and my hands flew up to his chest, as he towered over me and glowered at me.

"I came back in town early so that I could surprise you and take you to lunch, and this the type of shit that I find? I can't trust you, Tove?" His handsome face was all frowned up, as he looked down at me. I didn't know how to explain this shit because it did look bad.

"I swear it wasn't like that, Jahi. You know that you can trust me," I whined.

"Then what was it like?" He practically growled. I didn't know what to do because I could tell that he was angry and slipping into that version of himself that he was with Deon— that Hulk version. "Do I need to go out there and beat his ass and ask him what the fuck it's like?"

"No, Jahi." I wanted to tell him that he was acting crazy, but if the roles were reversed, then I probably would be to.

"Fire him."

"What?"

He tilted his head, as he peered down at me. I exhaled

sharply, before nodding my head. I would revisit the topic once he calmed down.

He took me by surprise when he leaned down and wrapped his arms around me, before capturing my mouth with his. He kissed me so hard and deep that my eyes fluttered shut, as our tongues danced.

"You missed me?" he asked, as he pulled back a little and stared into my eyes.

"Yes," I said breathily. And I wasn't lying. He had been gone for a week, handling business, and I missed him like crazy. I called him anytime that he texted and told me that he was free. And we FaceTimed until we fell asleep every night.

"Well, why you playing with me?" he asked with his face frowned up in pain, like I had done something to hurt him.

"I'm not. He came to bring me a drink, and I didn't know that he was going to ask me out. I hadn't really even had a conversation with him in forever besides it being work-related. The last time I talked to him was right before you proposed, and I was upset with you then. So... it's a misunderstanding."

His eyes roamed my face, as if he was trying to see if I was lying.

"I missed you too," he said, before he kissed me and groped my ass. My phone started to ring, and I knew it was the buyer. I pulled away and answered, confirming what I already knew.

"I'll be right back. Let me go sell this book," I told him,

and I chuckled when he groaned, before giving me another kiss and backing away.

"Wait," he stopped me, before pulling off the button-down that he had on. I didn't even resist, as he pushed back my bushy hair and brought it around me, before I stuck my arms into the sleeves. I watched, as he buttoned every button from my neck on down. "Go," he slapped my ass, before I walked away.

I had made a quick one-hundred and fifty thousand dollars by selling a first edition Ernest Hemingway, *In Our Time*. I was bringing the check to the safe in my office when I froze at the sight of Jahi sitting behind my desk flipping through the book. The GED prep book. I didn't tell anyone what I was studying for it because I didn't want to be embarrassed because I didn't have a diploma. His eyes met mine.

"This for you?"

I nodded. I went ahead and started to put the check in the safe.

"Why you ain't say shit?"

I sighed. "Because it's embarrassing. I'm twenty-three, and I don't have a diploma because my daddy sold me."

"It's fucked up, but it's not embarrassing."

I turned to look at him after locking the safe.

"Come here." He waved me over, and I just bit my bottom lip, as I took in his tall, muscular frame, as he relaxed in my office chair. He had on a black wife beater that was under the button up and some nice jeans and some kind of designer dress shoes.

I took a seat on the desk in front of him, and his hands flew to my thighs, and he started to massage up and down them. "Tove, you don't ever have to feel embarrassed with me. I want you to tell me about everything that's going on in your life. I want to know everything that I can about you, and I want to help you in any way that I can. You don't have shit to be embarrassed about, and I'm proud as fuck that you even want to do this shit. So many people would be satisfied with what you have and not try to better themselves. I'm proud of you, baby," he spoke, as he looked me in my eyes the whole time. Everything was just so different in my life after meeting Jahi. He paid attention to every little detail about me, and he wanted to offer anything that he could to help me and to make sure that I was happy.

"Thank you."

"It's just the truth." He scooted the chair closer, before kissing my lips. It was crazy to me how months had passed, and I still felt electricity when he touched me. The skin on my arms raised to form that Braille when he gripped my hips.

"I love you," I spoke against his lips, as his fingers reached into the waistband of my shorts.

"I love you too, but if you ever wear this shit again in public, I'mma fuck you up. Don't be around here displaying my shit, knowing damn well that you fine as fuck. About to get niggas fucked up." He fussed, as I lifted my eyes to the ceiling, before lifting my butt, so that he could pull my shorts down.

"What the fuck?" he asked, as he started to pull my shorts

down and underwear and got to the shoes that I had on. His upper lip formed a snarl.

"Don't start. I already had this argument with Khari earlier. I got them from Walmart."

"Nah. Hell nah," was all he said, before pulling the shoes off of my feet and throwing them into the office trash can. That's when I realized that his jealous ass threw away my hot cocoa too.

"Waitttt, those are my favorite ones," I whined, as he continued to pull my shorts off, before placing a hand on my chest and pushing me to lay back on the desk.

"You lucky I can't push them through the shredder," he mumbled.

"Hh!" I gasped, as his tongue swiped across my clit, and I automatically felt my juices start to flood. He eased two fingers inside of me, as he pulled my clit between his lips, and those shoes became a distant memory. My hands got entangled in his hair, as he ate me like he was starving, and I was the only thing that would fill him up.

"Jahi, please," I pleaded after my legs wouldn't stop shaking, and I was on the verge of blacking out from the third orgasm that was so powerful that I knew the whole bookstore had heard me moaning and calling out for mercy. I felt like that was exactly what he wanted, knowing that Daniel was right out front in the cafe.

"Bend over," he demanded, before snatching the shirt that I wore open and making the buttons fly everywhere. He quickly yanked the sports bra over my head. My eyes widened because I couldn't take any more.

"Jah—"

"Now."

I huffed, before bending over slowly on shaky, unsteady knees.

My fingers wrapped around the edge of the desk, and I whimpered when he slid his thick length deep inside of me, instantly causing a new set of orgasmic tremors.

"Fuckk!" He groaned, as he gripped my hips and started to pump into me rhythmically. I felt like my pussy was being abused by too much pleasure, as he ripped orgasms from my body over and over and over again. He was definitely punishing me for wearing this outfit out and the situation with Daniel. Our sexual dialect told it all. And he probably got the message that I loved the pressure that built in my belly from him constantly slamming into me, making our skin slick with sweat, as it slapped together. He came twice, before he finally stopped.

He trailed kisses up and down my spine, as I lay there, trying to catch my breath.

"You want to go to lunch?" he asked, as his voice vibrated against my skin and made me shiver.

"I want to go to sleep," I mumbled. He chuckled, before pulling back.

"Come on. Let's go home and get cleaned up and then we can go eat. I want to celebrate you starting your GED prep and you beating up them hoes that jumped you." He pulled

me up, and I stood there for a moment to steady myself,
before going to the bathroom that was in my office.

"Khari told you about that?" I queried.

"Craig told me about that. It's his job to tell me about
anything involving you."

"Mmm hmm. I need shoes," I called out from the bathroom, before he walked in behind me. I should've known that
Craig was going to say something when I talked about the
fight on the way here and he didn't say anything.

"I'll tell Craig to grab you some from Nike since that's
close," he said, before pecking my neck.

"All that so I won't wear shoes from Walmart?"

"The fuck I look like with all of the money and shit that I
have and my girl walking around here with some Velcro, crazy
house shoes on without the laces and shit? Nah." He shook
his head and started to kiss my neck more, wrapping his arms
around me, but I pulled away from him because he was just
trying to get stuff started back up.

I shook my head because he really made Craig go and get
me some Nike Vapor Max, before we could leave. It was
awkward as hell leaving the store with everybody knowing
what went down in my office, especially with me holding the
oversized button-down closed, since Jahi ripped the buttons
off. I didn't even look Daniel's way because I felt bad enough
that I was going to have to fire him the next day. I talked to
Jahi after sex, and he still wasn't having it. He felt like Daniel
was being disrespectful, especially since Jahi had been to the
store for me a few times since the day that he proposed.

"That was the walk of shame," I said once we were in the car and he started to drive with Craig trailing behind us.

"What? You were fucking your fiancé. Nobody better not tell you shit. And if they do, then call me. As a matter of fact, I'll drop you off myself tomorrow." I just stared at his profile to see if he was serious, and he was. I just decided to flick through the radio stations and enjoy the car ride home. It was pointless to object when he was going to do it anyway.

"You know anything about this?" I asked, as I shoved the newspaper into Jahi's face, as soon as I got downstairs.

"Nope," he said after he briefly glanced at the newspaper, before his eyes flew back to the TV screen and to the video game that he was playing.

"So, Daniel just mysteriously vanished and ended up in a newspaper article a few months after the incident at the store?"

"It seems so."

I just stared at him for a moment. I knew that he was lying to me. The next day after everything happened, Daniel never showed up to work for me to have the opportunity to fire him, and now a few months later, this.

"You ready, baby? Put that down." His eyes flowed to me again, before they ran amuck all over my body.

"No, because you're lying." I placed my hands on my hips, crumpling the paper in my hand. He stopped the game, throwing the controller to the side and standing up, before strolling over to me all smooth and shit like he was innocent. I took in how good he looked in the black tailored pants, black dress shirt with gold cufflinks, and nice black loafers with Medusa on them. I was almost sure that he said that everything he had on was Versace. I always loved when he wore black and how it contrasted against his caramel skin tone. His hair was in the neat low bun that he wore often. I caught a whiff of his cologne mixed in with his natural pheromones, and I fought to keep the glare on my face. He was one of those men that just naturally smelled good, and when he mixed cologne with that, the cologne never smelled the same as it did in the bottle—but even better.

"Baby, why are you worried about that? I told you that I didn't know anything about that." He pried the paper from my hand, before tossing it onto the sofa. "You look beautiful," he complimented, as he brushed the same mutinous curl out of my face that he always did; still having the ability to ignite my skin.

"Thank you." I tried to keep a serious face, but I couldn't help but to simper. I always felt giddy inside when he complimented me, and I would never understand that. "You look handsome."

"Thank you," he said, before pecking my lips. "Now let's

go, before we're late and we never hear the end of it from Khari."

"Alright." I grabbed my purse, before we headed out. Khari was having a dinner party tonight, and he had invited everyone. It wasn't an occasion for him or anything, so we didn't know what this was about.

When we pulled up to Khari's home, I couldn't do anything but stare and marvel at it, as I always did. While it was about the size of the home that I shared with Jahi, it was as grand as Khari's appearance. It was extravagant and over the top like his personality. He had a gold garden fountain of a woman in front of his home that lit up at nighttime. He had a three-story Mediterranean style mansion that was surrounded by lush plants, and it just looked so out of place in Gonzales, Louisiana.

Khari was extra and had way more housing attendants than Jahi. He had a valet out front and all. I grew nervous, as I accepted Jahi's awaiting hand while the valet waited to take his car. I knew that everyone had been invited, and that included his parents. Though he saw them regularly and wanted me to meet them again, I had declined, but this time I couldn't avoid them. His mama was a plain ol' bitch, and his dad wasn't that kind either from what I remembered. I understood their traditions, but they were outright calling me a whore in front of my face.

"Come on," Jahi pulled me to walk ahead of him, and I nervously did so.

"Mkuu!" I heard his father's voice boom as soon as we walked through the door. My body immediately stiffened, as Jahi wrapped a comforting arm around my waist. I would never get used to such a loud man.

His father was quick on his feet to be such a big man. He looked like a graying version of Jahi and Khari, but with a short haircut and a big belly.

"And Tove," he said softly, before snatching me up from Jahi and into a hug, crushing me. Shocked was an under-statement.

"Baba, back up, you're going to squish her," Jahi pulled me away with a chuckle, and I sharply inhaled to catch my breath.

He pulled away with a smile, before he grabbed my hands. "It is good to see you, daughter. I want to apologize for our last two encounters. I was confused about some things, but Jahi has now made them clear."

"A-all is forgiven, Mr. Nuru," I stuttered in shock, as I looked at the giant whose huge hands engulfed mine.

"You can call me Baba or Ayubu." He nodded, making me hesitantly do the same, before he released my hands and pulled Jahi into a bear hug.

I sighed when I saw his mother approaching us. She looked as if she was coming from the washroom in Khari's foyer.

Her beautiful cinnamon-colored skin glistened, as she strutted in our direction with her snub nose in the air and her hair wrapped in a beautiful purple headdress. Jahi's parents were nothing less than regal every time that I saw them. They looked like royalty.

"Jahi," she addressed him first, as he leaned down to give her a hug and kiss on the cheek.

"Toby," she said, as she looked down at me. Khari and Jahi had no choice but to be tall since their mother was tall too.

"Tove."

"Excuse me?" she said in her thick accent, face frowned up, feigning offense.

"My name is Tove. And I've spent way too long being called something else, to allow you to disrespect me and call me something different now."

Her hand clutched her chest.

"It was nice seeing you again, Ayubu and Mrs. Nuru." I gave a small grin, before I walked in the direction of the dining room. "What are you doing?" I asked Jahi once I felt his hand touch the small of my back. I thought that he would probably have to stay back and calm his mama down, since she looked so upset. I looked up into his face, and he was grinning down at me.

"Accompanying my fiancée." He looked ahead and pulled us into the dining room where all Khari's closest friends and associates were. There was an older couple there that I recognized from Ashley's crawfish boil.

It seemed like a pretty intimate dinner to say that Khari was making such a big deal out of everything.

"Where's Ashley?" I whispered to Aniya and Antony after Jahi and I took a seat next to Aniya.

"I don't know," they answered in unison, before looking at one another and rolling their eyes. They hated when they did that.

"Those are her parents though," Aniya pointed to the older couple and shrugged.

My eyebrows tented, as I looked toward Jahi, but he wasn't paying attention because he was looking at a menu and trying to choose from the two meal options that we had. We had the option to choose between a grilled chicken meal or a meal with steak.

It wasn't long before his parents joined us at the table and sat next to the older couple. They seemed like they knew each other well, as they chatted.

"I know that you all are probably wondering why you're gathered here today," Khari spoke from the top of the stair-well, making everyone look up at him. He was dressed in a black and white tuxedo.

"I thought that this wasn't formal." I leaned toward Jahi, before looking down at the black, long-sleeved, calf-length dress that I had on along with the black Saint Laurent Opyum heels.

"It's not." Jahi looked at his brother flatly, as he sat back in his seat and draped an arm across the back of my chair.

"Well, you are here because I wanted you to be the first that I announced my engagement to," he said, causing my mouth to fall open. I didn't know that he was seeing anyone seriously. His mother and father started to speak Swahili to one another, and Jahi just sat there looking dully.

Khari walked to the bottom of the stairs and then Ashley came out of a room next to the dining room while wearing a beautiful blue gown that hugged every curve.

"Wait," Antony and I said in unison, but Aniya just smiled.

"This is my fiancée." Khari gave a devious smirk, before kissing Ashley. The whole table was silent for a moment, as we all stared with our mouths agape. Well, everyone except Barika, Jahi, and Craig. Barika was praying, as she scurried back into the kitchen, Jahi seemed a little upset, and Craig looked pissed. I knew Khari talked shit about them being involved, but I had never witnessed it.

"Well, at least it is a woman." His father was the first to break the silence, before tossing his hands in the air and taking a sip of his wine.

"But why, Khari?" his mother asked incredulously.

Ashley's parents still had their mouths wide open. I had to join Jahi's father and take a sip of my wine.

"Because you and Baba were doing too much and were going to try to arrange my marriage. So, I pretended to be gay, so that I could take my time and find my own wife." He hunched his shoulders carelessly, before pulling out a chair for Ashley. This was just up their alley to be extra as hell.

His parents seemed rendered speechless at that. It was obvious that their tradition was no longer working for everyone.

"Well... congratulations." Ashley's mom smiled at them

brightly, making her father do the same. They seemed to like Khari at the crawfish boil, so I guessed that still stood to be true.

Everyone else fell in with giving them congratulations and everything, and eventually, even his parents came around. I felt a tinge of jealousy when his mother all of a sudden seemed so accepting of Ashley. Maybe they were just relieved that he wasn't gay. I had a feeling about him and Ashley a few times, but I dismissed it because of how Khari was. It made me wonder how much of it was an act and how much of it was him. It explained the kissing but not him kissing Aniya too.

Jahi and I both seemed wrapped up in our own thoughts during dinner, and after I congratulated Khari and Ashley, I was quiet. I figured that I'd never be able to completely escape my past.

"You alright?" Jahi leaned in and kissed my neck, as I nodded. I guess he sensed that I was a little bothered.

"Let me talk to you, Mkuu," Khari leaned down and told Jahi after dinner. Jahi quietly got up, still seeming a little annoyed, before following Khari.

Everyone else was talking and drinking and having a good time. I couldn't wait until Jahi got back, so that we could just go home and lay up in our own world. That was all that I really wanted today since I got up.

"Tove."

I fought a sigh when Jahi's mother approached me again and took his seat. At least she said my name correctly this time.

"Earlier, I didn't mean to upset you. I truly didn't know how to pronounce your name. I understand that you will be my daughter-in-law, whether I like it or not, so I want us to get along."

My eyes widened at her revelation.

"I was rude at first, and for that... I apologize. But I thought that you were taking an opportunity from a woman like me." Her manicured hand rested against her chest. "I didn't have much in Tanzania, before I came here and married Ayubu. And when I came here, I was very grateful. So, I wanted to make sure that my sons saw through with marrying women like their mother. I understand that I misjudged you and that you have a story, and maybe one day I can hear it." She looked at me expectantly, and I just nodded. I would never tell her my story. It was something that haunted me, and it also wasn't any of her business. But I could be cordial with her. I knew that even though Jahi did whatever he wanted, he was still very close to his family.

"It is nice to meet you, and I hope to see you more when we see Mkuu."

I was speechless, so I just nodded my head again, before she got up and touched my shoulder, before sauntering off. I just sat there stuck because his parents had done a complete three-sixty toward me.

"Come on, let's go," Jahi said while pulling me up from my seat all of a sudden.

"W-where are we going? I didn't get to tell Khari bye," I protested.

"Bye, gorgeous." Khari appeared out of nowhere, before shoving me along with Jahi. I quickly told everyone bye with Jahi's father crushing me in another hug. I was rushed out of the house, and valet was already waiting for us once we stepped outside.

"What's going on?" I asked once we got in the car, growing more and more nervous by the second.

"You'll see," was all Jahi replied, as he switched gears and sped down the road.

Chapter Seventeen

JAHI

"Let me talk to you, Mkuu," Khari leaned down and spoke. I got up, still irritated by his antics. I didn't care whether he was gay or not, but I didn't like the dishonesty. I considered my brother to be my best friend, but he obviously didn't see me the same. I felt like I didn't know him.

"No congratulations?" he asked while crossing his arms once we reached the foyer.

"Congratulations? Nigga, I don't even know who you are right now. Why would you keep something like that from me?" I frowned.

"Jahi, because it wasn't about you, and honestly, would you have approved of me acting gay so that I could avoid the bull-shit that you went through?" He cocked his head to the side with pursed lips.

"Nah. Not exactly. But I would've eventually supported you. Got me feeling like I don't know you and shit. Was this all an act?" I waved my hand, not at anything in particular.

"What? Hell no." He grimaced. "I'm still me. I'm still the exact same person. I just don't like niggas. Never have. I actually *love* pussy. Shit is a fucking delicacy," he was speaking to me but it looked as if his mind was somewhere else.

"Then what about all that shit with Craig? And if you're marrying Ashley, then why you kissing Aniya?" I was confused as fuck.

"Oh, nah. That nigga Craig is gay. He approached me because he thought I was, but I turned him down and told him he wasn't my type. He was embarrassed, so he let me say whatever I wanted about him. And Aniya? Ashley and I have fun with her together. She's the only one who knew about Ashley and me." He shrugged.

I just took a second to process everything and take him in, and everything was the same. He still had the same mannerisms and all. The nigga just wasn't gay. I shrugged and shook my head. I didn't understand him going so far out of his way, but whatever. I remembered when we were younger and how people assumed Khari was gay because of how he acted. I guess he used being metropolitan sexual, or whatever the fuck it's called, to his advantage.

"Congratulations, Khari. If you're happy, then you know that I'm happy for you."

"Thank you, Mkuu." He grinned while staring somewhere else. My eyes followed his, and he was staring at Ashley, as she talked to everyone. I did a double take when I saw my mama talking to Tove, and everything looked fine. I knew that my mama wanted to apologize, but her initial delivery was off, so I was going to let it be until she tried again. Just like my father stood behind her, I was going to stand behind Tove with any decision that she made on the situation, since they were so rude initially. My mama had some snobby ways to say that she came from the background that she did, but she wasn't all bad at all.

"Y'all using protection, Mkuu? Tove is getting thick, as hell," he asked. Now knowing that he wasn't gay, I gave his ass the side-eye, before he smacked my shoulder. "Nigga, not like that! I buy her damn clothes, and I was wondering if her ass was pregnant."

"Nah. She's on birth control. Has been for months." I tilted my head, as I glanced at her, and her face was getting a little rounder. I shrugged.

"I remember the first night that we took her from Slim, and I was excited as hell. You know what I had told everyone just off meeting her that one time?"

"Hmm?"

"That Mkuu had found his wife. Ain't that some shit?"

I smirked, as I studied her. "Yeah, it is. Some true shit."

"Mkuu!" Khari exclaimed all of a sudden.

"What nigga?"

"It's seven thirty." He tapped his watch, making me jump into action with getting Tove and leaving. I had plans for us, and we couldn't miss this shit.

She looked scared as hell from the passenger seat, as I switched lanes. It took about twenty-five minutes from Khari's house, but we still got there in time.

"Hh!" She gasped once we pulled to the front of the building. I rounded the car to help her out, before dropping my keys into the hands of valet. "How did you know that I wanted to come here?" she asked, as she marveled at the opera house, Opéra Louisiane.

"I pay attention to my woman. And what better day to bring you to see your favorite play than your birthday?" I looked down at her, as we were escorted to the balcony. She looked at me with low, worried eyes. "I'm not mad. I'm disappointed that you thought that I wouldn't figure out your birthday after all of this time, and I just want to know why you didn't tell me? You're going to be my wife." The one time I had asked, she quickly changed the subject.

Her eyes roamed around the building in amazement, before they came back to me. "Because it never mattered before. I guess I have a little PTSD because the past birthdays that Slim gave me were torture. Also, with you, a birthday didn't even matter because every day feels like the perfect birthday. And I didn't want to make a big deal out of anything. It's just another day." She lifted her left shoulder.

"Well, everything should be a big deal when it's pertaining to you," I told her, before the doors were opened for us and we were escorted to our seats. I hated that she felt that way and made a mental note to change it. She was a simple person that didn't require much to be happy, but that wasn't her being simple. That was a reflection of her past.

I chuckled when her eyes widened when Juliet appeared on stage. She was obsessed with the story of Romeo and Juliet, so I brought her to see Roméo et Juliette. I didn't understand the hype because I thought it was a fucked-up love story, but she loved it. Tove had a dark side that appealed to tortured works of art.

I had no choice but to watch her, as she watched the opera. She was beautiful, and I don't know if I had ever seen her eyes so light and expressive. I leaned toward her and kissed her temple, as she wiped the single tear that cascaded down her cheek after the final act.

"That was beautiful." Her thick accent drawled every word slowly.

"The shit is kind of weird to me, but you enjoyed it, so sure." She gave me a cute frown, before hitting my arm.

I tried hard not to tell her to shut up when we were back in the car because she was telling me every scene of the show like I wasn't there. Granted, I wasn't watching it much, but I got the gist. I loved hearing her voice, but Tove could talk a nigga's head off when she was in the mood.

"Wait, this isn't the direction of home." She finally stopped talking about that show.

"Nope," I said, as we pulled up to the airport.

"Are we going somewhere?" she asked with her eyes ballooned, making me chuckle.

"Eventually. Let's go check it out." I rounded the car and helped her out, before helping her onto the private jet. She gawked at the sight of the inside with the cream leather seats and mahogany furniture.

"Are those for me?" She looked back at me while pointing at the gifts wrapped in blue gift wrap. I nodded. I took a seat and watched, as she stalked toward the bags, before sitting across from me to open them.

"Baby, hurry up." I leaned forward to put a present in her lap. She was moving in slow motion.

"I'm not used to this. Leave me alone." She rolled her eyes at me.

She finally started to peel the paper off of the flat rectangular gift, before she pulled it completely free of paper, and a bright smile covered her face.

"That's from Aniya and Antony." I pointed.

"It's beautiful. I think I'll hang it in the store." Her fingers ran across the white frame of the picture of her side profile from her interview with *Melanated Magazine*.

"Well, I'm going to get another one for the house."

She blushed, before placing the picture to the side and grabbing a box.

"A bad bitch, for a bad bitch," she read the note from Khari, and I just shook my head.

"Oh, shit!" I almost jumped out of my seat when she squealed and pulled the small gun out of the box. She still couldn't shoot too well, and this nigga bought her a gun.

"Oh, look! It's blue! And calm down. It's not loaded... pussy." She mumbled that last part, as I leaned forward and took the gun from her and placed it back into the box.

"Khari out of his fucking mind." I fussed, as she rolled her eyes, before getting to Ashley's gift that was a first edition book that she had personally wanted.

"Now from me," I told her while reaching to give her a gold folder.

She hesitantly took it from me, before opening it and studying the contents.

"I don't get it. What is it? Is it the deed to something?" She looked up at me.

"The deed to this jet. Turns out you're incredibly hard to shop for. What do you buy a woman that doesn't want anything? You don't want a bigger house, you don't want a car, you don't want another bookstore, you hardly spend any money that you make from the bookstore, and you never really ask for anything. But then I thought about it and how you're always reading travel magazines and books about foreign places, so I bought you a jet so that we could go to those places anytime that you want. In three days, we leave for Verona, and since you're obsessed with Romeo and Juliet, I figured that would be first on your list. Your name will be on the side of the jet by then."

She just stared at me with tears clouding her eyes, before she blinked, and tears rushed down her cheeks.

"I hope those are happy tears." I chuckled nervously. I

didn't know if I went too big since she was so simple. She said nothing, as she put the folder aside and rushed to me to straddle my lap and hug me. Her face buried into my chest, as her body trembled.

"Thank you so much. I love it. I—I never had anyone like you. I never really understood why or how I got you or what happened to offset the cosmic balance in the universe and caused us to meet that day. But I'm so grateful that it did. And the more and more that I fall in love with you, the more I consider there being a God."

I hate to admit it, but that shit made my eyes glaze over.

"You didn't get me; I got blessed with you. You think that I somehow saved you, but I never realized that my life was so dull and monotonous until I found you. You challenged me like I've never been challenged before, and you immediately made me fall for you, fast and hard. I'm not my normal selfish self when I'm with you. I'm somehow a better man and a better person. You've humbled me in some ways and changed me. I love you, Tove."

"I—I love you too," she cried into my chest, as her body shook. I didn't even see her cry like this after her encounter with her father. I rubbed her back and held her until she settled down and pulled away to look me in my face. She leaned forward and kissed me hard and deep as hell.

When she pulled back, I wiped her face with my thumbs, as I just stared at her. She looked around, before looking back at me.

"They gon' have Patrón on here?" she randomly asked, making me titter, as I nodded.

"Fucking alcoholic," I spoke against her lips, before kissing her again. She had to chuckle herself at that.

"Baby, I've never been out of Louisiana. I damn sure can't ride no jet without a drink," she fussed, making me laugh at how lively her personality could be at times. Sometimes we both could just exist in complete silence and be satisfied, and other times she was live as hell.

"You ready to go home?" I asked, as she sighed, before nodding.

"Honestly, that's how I wanted to spend my birthday, laid up with you. But you made it so much better." She stood up from my lap, before looking at me like she was confused. "You ever had sex on a jet?"

"Can't say that I have," I answered honestly with my hands roaming up her thick thighs, already catching her drift. I was always ready to go with her.

I chuckled, as she wiggled her eyebrows at me, before dropping to her knees.

"Shouldn't this be the other way around?"

"Unt un," she said distractedly as she unzipped my pants. I think her ass just enjoyed hearing me moan all loud and shit while trying to get away from her demon ass. But I wasn't going to object either. Tove gave that dome doctor, gulp-gulp, twist, pump three thousand head. Her ass treated my dick like a Bop It.

I brushed her hair from her face, making her eyes flow up to me. They were no longer the eyes that I saw last year in May. They were light like she was happy, and they looked hopeful. They confirmed that every choice that I had ever made concerning her was right.

Chapter Eighteen

TOVE

V erona was beautiful. We had been back for a month, and I felt like I was still swooning in and feeling the love from the city. We hit all of the major landmarks that I saw in travel magazines, and we even stood on Juliet's balcony. Jahi said that it was a load of tourist bullshit, but I thought that it was beautiful.

Jahi: Baby, bring ya ass so that you can change and we can leave. I'm fucking starving.

I shook my head, as I read the text from Jahi. Tonight was the night that I was supposed to meet his whole family, and I was not looking forward to it. I didn't have any problems with them or anything, but Jahi had a huge family. Meeting so many people at one time was going to be overwhelming.

After his parents stood their ground on behalf of us and Khari and Ashley, the family finally accepted the fact that we were getting married, which apparently wasn't too hard since Jahi's father was kind of like the Big Kahuna. What exactly did their family do? I wasn't clear on all of that. I just knew that sometimes Jahi left for a week or so, before coming back home and that they for sure got taxes from businesses, as if they were the government.

Tonight was to celebrate both of our engagements at his parents' house, and Barika had left to go help the other house attendants. And while I was happy for the sake of Jahi's relationship with his family that they accepted us being together, I wasn't exactly rushing home either.

Me: I made some beanie weenies last night. Eat that.

I responded, before chuckling. I knew that he was going to say something snobbish. I was going to head out as soon as I got my GED in the mail. It was coming to the bookstore since I used this address when starting the classes. I knew I could've gotten it later, but I wanted to receive it in my own hands. It was a big deal to me, and after talking to Jahi, I no longer felt embarrassed.

"Thank you." I grinned when I met the mail carrier at the door and got the envelope. I didn't even wait for a response, as I rushed back into the store and ripped it open, before pulling out the contents. There was my GED with Tove Monroe embossed on it in gold. I ran my index finger across my name, and I couldn't help the smile that crept across my face. Since I had accomplished this, I was going to get ready to take the SATs, so that I could apply for college.

I wanted to be a social worker so that I could try and help girls like me. Maybe I would be able to spot them in public with their abuser and just be able to tell. I believed that we had a look. I believed that we all had either dead or pleading eyes.

"Hi, uh, yes. I'm looking for a Tove Monroe. I heard that she works here," I heard from behind me. I spun around to find a pretty brown-skinned woman with a huge shiny afro and deep-set eyes being pointed in my direction by the new barista.

"Can I help you?" I asked, as I looked her up and down. She was beautiful, and I was praying that she wasn't here to ruin my day. Life was funny like that for me. Things would be going great, and then tragedy would follow.

"Tove, it's me. Anna," she said, as my eyes fell to the floor, as they quickly went left to right while I tried to match her new, grown up face with the name.

"Annabelle?" I asked with wide eyes.

She smiled brightly, then nodded. "Well, I prefer to just go by Anna now. Annabelle seems so... dated," she spoke in an accent thicker than mine while using her hands, just like she did when we were kids.

"How did you find me?" I asked, as I stood there stuck in place.

"Well, your daddy supposedly married a woman named Coral. She wrote a letter to us, and maybe she wrote one to your daddy's side, as well. I got the letter, and I just had to come see you. Can I get a hug or something? You got me feeling all nervous and shit." She chuckled awkwardly, as I nodded.

I quickly swiped at the single tear that ran down my face, as I hugged her back. She was the daughter of my uncle, who'd been killed. She was my childhood confidant, and we were ripped apart when we were ran out of town.

"You're just as beautiful as I remember. Is this store for you? It's beautiful," she asked, as she pulled away from me and looked at the picture of me from *Melanated Magazine* on the wall.

"Uh. Y-yeah. Thanks," I told her, before her eyes flowed back to me. She looked at me for a second, before her eyes started to well, and she rushed me with another hug.

"I'm so sorry. I just missed you so much, Tove. I looked for you all over on social media, but I never could find you." She pulled away and grabbed my hands.

"Yeah, I never got into social media. How have you been?" I asked, as I just stood there in shock. I wasn't going to tell her that I hadn't had a normal life until now. And I didn't know how to thank Coral since I didn't have anything on my daddy. Anna rambled on and on and mentioned how she had two children and a husband and how they just moved out of the bayou and lived in Gonzales now. She had gotten the letter right before she left. That was really good to hear because that meant that she wasn't far away from me. She told me how we had a few cousins that were still around, but a lot of our older family members had passed away. My grand-mother and grandfather died shortly after we left Delacroix.

"Oh, and I'm so sorry, Tove. I'm sorry for your loss." She broke my train of thought, making me frown.

"Say what now?"

"Your father. I never really liked his family, but Mark was alright. I heard that he died and that his funeral was back home a week ago. Did you go?" she asked, face etched in concern.

"N-no. We weren't very close." I made the understatement of the century.

"I'm sorry to hear that. They said that him and some woman that wasn't his wife were murdered together in his home. Apparently, Coral had left him and went out of state when she sent the letter. Didn't even get a chance to divorce him good. I'm sorry. I know how hard losing a father can be on a girl." For some reason, his death had Jahi written all over it. I didn't know how to feel. I wasn't angry. I stopped being sad a few weeks after I saw him, and I told myself that he was dead like I originally thought. So, now that it rang true, I was more indifferent than upset. And honestly, with Jahi, I was surprised it hadn't happened sooner.

I gave her sad eyes of my own at the mention of her father, but she shrugged and gave me a bright smile. "I'm just so happy to have my favorite cousin back. We were as thick as thieves. Hell, we were thieves."

I chuckled at the memory of us constantly stealing candy from a corner store and running out. We got in trouble every time, but that never stopped us.

"Tove Monroe!" she shouted my name, making me jump.

My eyes followed hers, as her thumb ran across my engagement ring. "This is beautiful. Are you engaged?"

I nodded and smiled, before it occurred to me that I was late as hell.

"Oh, shit. Anna, can I get your number so that we can catch up later? I'm actually late to something with my fiancé." I felt bad that I had to leave, but I checked my phone and realized that twenty minutes had already passed. I also noticed that Jahi never texted me back.

"Oh, that's no problem. I have to get back to this hungry husband and these kids of mine anyway." She waved me off, before we exchanged numbers and another hug.

"Craig, I don't want to hear it. I know I'm late," I held my hand up, as he opened the door for me. He had a worried expression on his face, but that wasn't new when dealing with Jahi.

It was odd to me though how his eyes kept glancing from the road back to me in the rearview mirror. I tried to call Jahi to see if he was upset, but I got no answer.

"Hello?" I answered the phone for Khari, as we pulled up to our home.

"Ma'am, where the hell are y'all? Y'all are late, and the Nuru family doesn't do late," he fussed, as I rolled my eyes and grabbed my keys from my purse.

"I know, I know. It's my fault—" my voice trailed off, and I dropped my phone after I realized that the door was already slightly ajar. I glanced back at Craig, and he wore a weird expression that I couldn't read.

"Jahi!" I called out after I quickly pushed the door open, and I lost my breath at the sight. Slim was standing in the foyer over Jahi's body that had a wound in his chest.

"Lovie," Slim cooed. "I heard that you were talking, but I didn't believe it." I couldn't take my eyes off of Jahi, as I stalked toward him. "Lovie what are you doing?" Slim caught me from falling to my knees on the ground beside him. He was unconscious, and it didn't look like he was breathing.

"Let me go!" I screamed, as I fought against him.

POW!

I froze and backed away from Slim, as I heard him fire a gun. I turned around to see that he had shot Craig right between his eyes.

"That nigga was sneaky. He was the one who found me lurking around, but he didn't tell the Nuru family because he wanted me to help him get revenge on that gay nigga that apparently ain't gay. He said that I was the only one that had snuck under the Nuru's radar for so long. I told him I'd help him if he helped me. That Ashley girl was next, but I just wanted to handle this nigga, get you, and go. I told you that I was coming for you, Lovie. I missed you so much, baby. But you got a lot of making up to do. I lost my sister and my baby because of you. I gave up everything so that I could come back for you." He sounded deranged, and I cringed, as he walked up on me and wrapped an arm around my waist. My eyes snapped shut and he sniffed my hair.

"O-okay. Let me just get a few things," I stuttered, as I felt him nod against my neck, before he kissed me there. It took him a minute, as he kissed on my neck and the side of my face repeatedly, but he let me go. I stalked toward my purse that was on the ground, before picking it up and quickly pulling out my gun that Khari bought me. I wasn't even supposed to carry it today, but we had an impromptu lesson this morning, before I went to the bookstore. I was quick on my pivot, as I turned around and pointed the gun toward Slim.

"L-lovie, w-what the fuck are you doing?" he asked, raising his hands in surrender. "Don't tell me you let this African motherfucka brainwash you! I love you! I came back for you! I killed this piece of shit for you, and I lost Miranda for you, you stupid bitch!" He kicked Jahi's leg, as he ranted.

Click! POW!

I cocked the gun and sent off the first round into his chest, the same as he had done Jahi. He looked down at his chest, before looking back up at me with tears falling from his eyes. He staggered, as his body fell into the wall of the foyer.

"L-lovie please—"

"My name is *Tove!*" I screamed, as tears clouded my vision.

Click! POW!

I sent the final round between his eyes, before I dropped the purse that I still held onto and ran to Jahi's side. My shaky hand couldn't feel a pulse when I checked his neck.

Jahi Ife Nuru. It means dignity, love and light. And Slim had just taken away the person who instilled into me dignity, the person who showed me the most love, and the person that brought me light. I didn't care about anything, as I kneeled next to his body, as the blood pooled underneath it and drenched my clothes and stained my skin.

I leaned down and kissed both of his closed eyes, his nose and then his lips. He was still warm. I could tell that his spirit hadn't left long ago. I figured maybe I could catch up, as the tears cascade down my face.

I brought the gun to my head in a trembling hand. I was a fool to think that I could've ever been truly happy. That there might've been a God that somehow saw me or cared about me like Jahi believed that there was.

Click!

My emotions and the time that I got to be Tove left, as I cocked the gun and closed my eyes. Maybe this was the only way that bitch Lovie would finally leave too. I loved how I had finally told Jahi about the nickname, yet he never let it flow from between his lips.

"Hhhhhh," I heard him gasp and suck up all of the available oxygen in the room while I exhaled everything that I had to lend to him. I sobbed with my eyes closed.

I felt his still warm fingers grab my arm that held the gun.

This can't be real, my mind is fucking with me, I thought. *This is some kind of fucked up survival tactic.*

I felt his grip pulling my arm and the gun away from my head, and I slowly peeled open my laden eyes that felt like they did the night I was sold for an eighth, as I looked down into the eyes of my dignity, love and light.

"It's real," I whispered.

I stared into his reddened, low eyes, and, before I could

spring to action, the door was burst further open, as his family filled the room.

"Come on, Tove," I heard Ashley mumble in my ear, as she tried to help me up, but I was planted by his side. Jahi's eyes closed again, and his hand dropped from my arm, before Khari blocked my view and lifted his brother up. Khari's face was stern, as he swiftly carried Jahi away. I reached out for him, as I sat in the puddle of his blood and sobbed. "Come on, baby. Let them handle this. Let's get you cleaned up." Ashley hugged me, as my eyes snapped shut and I sobbed into her chest. This was all my fault. I shouldn't have been here. I should've run away from Jahi so that he could be safe. I knew that nothing but pain and heartbreak followed me. I knew what happened when I thought that I could be happy.

"Please let me go, Ashley. I can't do this without him." I cried, as Ashley pried the gun out of my hand. She held onto me tighter, as I cried until I got a migraine. Everyone else in the room moved around us and started to clean things up, but they all faded into the background. Ashley sat there with me for longer than I could remember, as I sobbed. Nothing would ever be the same if Jahi didn't somehow pull through. I needed that more than I needed my own breath in my lungs.

EPILOGUE

Tove

THREE MONTHS LATER

I laid in Jahi's spot in the bed and inhaled his scent that still lightly lingered there. My hand flew to my protruding belly, as my baby kicked. Tears sprung to my eyes, as I thought back on how I had almost killed myself and the piece of Jahi that I had growing inside of me. I found out that I was two months pregnant when I almost took my and *his* life. Turns out that my birth control had failed.

I quickly closed my eyes to divert the tears when I heard the bedroom door open. I knew that he was probably about to fuss. I spent a good portion of my time laying here in this spot.

"No ma'am. Get your ass up. We aren't doing this today, Tove." Khari fussed at me, as I kept my back turned to him. I heard him blow out a frustrated breath, before I felt a dip in the bed. I slowly turned around to face him, as he laid beside me. "Tove, it's been three months. I know that it's still bothering you and honestly, it fucks with me too because it was about me, but we have to try to move on," he spoke, as my pointer finger ran across his sharp jawline. He had shaved his beard and mustache, and it looked so funny to me. He was still handsome, but it was odd.

"I can't forgive myself, Khari," I told him, as the tears rushed to my eyes again, but this time they fell. He sighed, before he reached up and swiped them away.

"Tove, you been through a lot of shit, so I can understand why you feel that way, but nobody is blaming you for what happened. You have this baby coming in four months, and you have to pull yourself together, mama." He rubbed my arm, as my lips quivered, and I fought back the tears while nodding. We laid there for a few more minutes so that I could gather myself.

"Where is Ashley?" I finally spoke up. A cute grin crossed Khari's lips, as it always did when anyone brought her up.

"She's with my mama and everyone else picking out wedding dresses." I immediately felt sad again. "Come with me. I have something to show you." He intervened, before I could start crying again.

"Okay." I slowly pulled myself from the bed.

"Ma'am, the hairstylist is coming over in an hour because your hair is flat as hell, and it's way longer than you normally keep it."

I ran a hand over my hair, and Khari was right. I hadn't cared to get a haircut in a while, so it was well down my back and very heavy, so it wasn't, as fluffy.

"Shit!" I hissed, as I opened the bedroom door and the new butler zoomed by me.

"Sorry, Tove!" he called out over his shoulder.

"I'll never get used to having so many people here just to cater to me." I fussed, as Khari grabbed my hand and pulled me along with him.

"You know Jahi wouldn't have it any other way." He threw over his shoulder. "Look." He moved to the side, as we approached the doorway to the baby's room.

"Hh!" I gasped at the sight of the beautiful baby bed that was made from the first bookshelf that Jahi had ever made for me. I teared up, as my eyes fell to the built-in bookshelf and the baby books that were under the crib. This held so much meaning to me. The bookshelf represented a new beginning for me, and now that same wood was being used to represent another new beginning with my baby.

"I hope those are happy tears."

My eyes flew to Jahi, as he finished tightening a screw in, before rising to his full height. I nodded, before rushing to hug him. He chuckled and kissed my forehead. "What took y'all so long?" he asked, as I pulled away from him a little and looked up into his handsome face.

"Her ass was laying in your spot doing all of that crying. Same as she does every day." Khari fussed, and I shot him a glare, before giving him the bird.

"Baby, you've been all on my ass and depressed ever since that day. I told you that yo' ass wasn't getting away from me that easy. God gave a nigga an extra life just for you and my son," he said, as he looked into my eyes, and I started to cry again.

"Oh, Mungu!" Khari yelled out to the Lord, before walking off. I felt bad for not being there for Ashley while she picked out dresses today, but I had a hard time leaving the house most days. Ashley and I had truly become sisters because even on the days where I didn't say much, she would still sit with me and watch TV or whatever I decided to do.

"Baby, come here." Jahi pulled me into his lap in the white oak rocking chair next to the baby bed. My eyes roamed the royal blue and gold room, and I looked at the letters of the baby's name that were on the wall. "What I told you about all of that? You do that every time that I leave the house. I told you I was coming right back," he said, as I laid my head on his chest.

"I know but *still*." The events that took place and me being pregnant made me extra emotional. Jahi had been shot in the chest, but by some miracle, it had missed his vital organs. He was able to come home two weeks after being shot, and I was in his back pocket ever since. And whenever he had to leave the house, like to go pick up the crib from his workshop, I got really upset.

"But still what? I'm here, Tove, and your little gangsta ass took out the nigga that we were looking for. I'm pissed that him and that nigga Craig caught me off guard and ran down on me, but you handled that, and I'm grateful for that. Stop being hard on yourself. My life means so much more to me now that I have you and my son." He grabbed my chin and lifted my head. "You hear me?"

"Yes," I told him, before he kissed my lips.

"Have you packed anything for our trip next week?"

"Now you know that Khari did all of that for me."

"True." He chuckled.

In a week, we were leaving, and we were staying in Tanzania until I gave birth. We had decided that after everything that took place that we needed to get away for a while, and to what better place than the motherland? We were going to get married there, as well, and I was excited to get married and have my baby in Africa. Jahi just had to finish tying up some loose ends and finishing the baby bed was the final one. Ashley and Khari were going to run the bookstore for me, while I was gone, and I trusted no one more than those two. They had already been helping with it a lot, since I didn't leave the house much.

When I got back, I planned on spending a lot of time with Anna and catching up with her. I hadn't seen Anna since that day three months ago, but after I told her what had happened, she understood and gave me space. We still talked on the phone twice a week though.

I was happy to have some family of my own in my life. The other family that we had in the bayou still held onto the family rivalry, so they didn't want to meet, but I was okay with that. I never knew if my daddy's side of the family got a letter or not because they never reached out. I asked Jahi once if he knew anything about him being murdered, but he denied it. I didn't ask anymore because I knew that if he did, he would never admit to it.

"So, how do we say his name in Cajun-French again?" he asked, eyebrows dipped, as my eyes roamed his face.

"T-Jahi. T basically means junior but instead of saying it after the name you say it in front of it."

"T-Jahi?"

"Mmm hmm." I hummed, as I took his appearance and presence in. I felt horrible that I almost killed myself and my baby, and I still felt like I had somehow caused the incident. But I was slowly working my way past that with the therapist that I had started to see. Jahi felt like me trying to kill myself again was the tip of the iceberg and that it was time that I finally sought help. I would continue our sessions via Face-Time once I left.

"I love you, Jahi Ife Nuru," I told him for what I was sure was the fifth time that day.

"And I love you, Tove Monroe Nuru." He kissed my lips again. He never got upset on the days that I told him that I loved him a lot. He didn't even get upset on the days that I was all under him. He understood how that must've been for me to see him like that and under those circumstances.

I laid my head on his chest and closed my eyes, while trying to burn this memory of us sitting there into my mind. Not because I felt like we'd never have another intimate moment, but because when we returned, we'd be here with a new addition.

He started to rub up and down my back, as we both embraced that silence that we both appreciated. I thought back to the night that I was sold and how bad things were, before that day that he saved me. Before the incident, the way that everything happened and how Jahi saw me at the perfect time, before I could be taken away had me often revisiting the idea of there being a God. But when I thought about that deep breath that Jahi took, I was pushed into being a full-on believer. On top of that, I was mostly happy. Besides some guilt, I was comfortable, I was taken care of, I was loved, and I was bringing a life into this world. I even gained a whole new family while connecting back with a family member of my own. And when we got back and got settled in with our baby, I'd be starting college.

"Excuse me, love birds, the hairstylist is here," Khari interrupted, making me sigh, as my eyes peeled open. I was quickly whisked away like it was my third day there all over again. Khari had a stylist there, a nail tech, and a hairstylist. I would be lying if I said that I didn't miss getting pampered like this every week. Khari had me spoiled with the weekly house visits, before three months ago. Once they were finished, I stood in the mirror and looked myself over in the black, thin-strapped fitted dress that hugged my belly in a comfortable way. I stepped into the nude sandals and studied my hair that was now bouncy and back at my shoulders.

"Whew, chile! Tove is that you? I surely thought a bum bitch had taken over your life," Khari said from the doorway, as I gave him the finger.

"Whew, gay Khari, is that you? I surely thought a straight man had taken over your life," I quipped, and his eyes widened, before he smirked.

"The bitch is back."

I laughed at his remark because I did feel like myself again. Self-care definitely helped with that.

"You look beautiful, baby. You ready?" Jahi asked, before handing the butler his bottle of water, as he waited downstairs by the door for me. We had moved into a new house since I had a hard time living in the other one. We were on our way to finally have that engagement party with his family. This was also a party for them to see us off, before we left. I actually met them during Jahi's time in the hospital, and they were all very sweet to me. They didn't seem bothered that it was my relationship with Slim that had landed him there. They sort of felt like if he had the proper security then that situation would've been prevented.

"Yup." I briefly closed my eyes and took a deep breath, as he brushed a curl from my face. "Do you feel that?" I finally asked.

"What?"

"When you touch me, do you feel anything?" I just had to

know. So much time had passed, and the feeling never went away.

He nodded with a smirk. "It's like electricity."

My cheeks warmed at his acknowledgement. "Yeah. That's what I feel too," I told him, before raising to the tip of my toes for a kiss that still made my skin raise in Braille. We were silent, as he let me in the passenger seat of his car, before getting in himself. I broke out into a grin, as he let the top down just like I loved, and I got to feel my hair blowing in the wind. I simpered, as Jahi lifted my hand to his lips and kissed the back of it.

When we pulled up to the huge mansion, I was no longer surprised by the appearance or how large it was. There was already staff waiting outside for us, as valet took Jahi's car and we were greeted immediately by a butler.

"Daughter," Jahi's mother, Hediye, sauntered toward me with a bright smile and open arms. She looked beautiful in her blue, yellow, and black headdress with the matching khanga. I hugged her, as her hands went up and down my back, before she pulled back, and her hands flew to my stomach, as they always did. She had been clinging on to me ever since Jahi was in the hospital. She felt like if something had happened to her son that I was all that she would have left of him, and she wanted to love me because he did.

"How is my grandson?"

"Active." I rolled my eyes, making her let out an airy laugh.

"Exactly like his Baba."

"Tove!" Ayubu thundered, causing me to jump. I couldn't

get used to that for the life of me. I think I even felt my son kick at the sound of his grandfather's voice.

"Baba, chill," Jahi fussed, as he pried me away from one of his father's crushing hugs. Ayubu waved him off, before rubbing my stomach, as well and asking about his first grandson. Their whole family was very intimate, and I was terrified that they were going to spoil T-Jahi to death.

"They like you more than me now," Jahi whispered, making me chuckle. Even though I knew that it wasn't true, it did seem that way. They came to our home and invited us to theirs all the time.

"Dinner is this way, daughter," Heyedi grabbed my hand and pulled me along with her.

"Hh!" I gasped, as my hands flew to my mouth. I saw Anna, her husband Croix, Aniya, Antony, Ashley, Khari, and Jahi's whole family gathered around a table that was adjacent to a table that was piled with nothing but gifts. This was a surprise baby shower, and I was in awe, as I saw the huge room decorated in blue and gold just like T-Jahi's bedroom. Everything was fit for a prince.

"Y'all!" I whined, tearing up immediately.

"Y'all!" Almost everyone mocked me.

"I don't get it," Anna said with a cute frown on her face, making us all laugh. She was more country than me, so she didn't understand them mocking me at all.

It wasn't long, before I was pulled away from Jahi and sitting in the midst of everyone while talking and eating Tanzanian food. My favorite was the mandazis.

"I'm sorry that I missed dress shopping with you earlier," I sincerely apologized to Ashley who sat at my side. It was like the room had divided between men and women.

"Tove, we didn't go dress shopping. I was here the whole time getting everything together for you. We're doing that tomorrow, even if I have to bring the dresses to your house to try on in front of you. You know damn well that I wouldn't let you miss that," she sassed.

"True," I said after thinking on it for a second. Ashley was dead set on me being her Matron of Honor and was purposely waiting for me to give birth and get married to do so.

After talking to everyone, I was finally able to break free for a second and slide into Jahi's lap, as he sat to himself at the gift table and snooped through the gift bags, before I could open them.

"Why are you snooping?" I asked with a raised eyebrow, as he gave me that cute smirk. I ran my hand across his hair, before squeezing the bun at the back of his head.

"I'm trying to see if we got anything good. We need that new diaper genie."

I shook my head and tittered because he was so ready to be a father that he researched shit on the internet all night while we laid in bed.

I turned around in his lap and got comfortable to watch everyone enjoy themselves and mingle. Jahi kissed the side of my face, as his large hands roamed to my belly, and I briefly closed my eyes to bask in the ambience, before I could be pulled away again.

There had to be somebody bigger than me out there, moving time and space for me to be saved from the situation that I was in to bring me to where I am now.

After everything that took place, I no longer romanticized tortured love stories or *any* love story for that matter, as I focused and devoted more time on building my own happy and healthy one. After all, this was no ordinary love.

CPSIA information can be obtained
at www.ICGtesting.com
Printed in the USA
LVHW081803081020
668326LV00015B/1950